by the same author

I COULD RIDE ALL DAY IN MY COOL BLUE TRAIN

The Short Day Dying

PETER HOBBS

faber and faber

First published in 2005
by Faber and Faber Limited
3 Queen Square London WC1N 3AU
This paperback edition published in 2006

Typeset by Faber and Faber
Printed in England by Mackays of Chatham plc, Chatham, Kent

A CIP record for this book
is available from the British Library

ISBN 978-0-571-21718-2
ISBN 0-571-21718-4

For my father, in memory

I went to the garden of love,
And saw what I never had seen:
A chapel was built in the midst,
Where I used to play on the green.

William Blake

THE SHORT DAY DYING

Another Sabbath is gone into eternity borne from us swiftly as though the angels gathered it in their arms flung wide to harvest the days. Our time is stolen from us and we are blind to its loss neither will we see it again mine hours have been wasted. The days flicker with light and are quickly past.

In the short hours today I made my labours though they left me tired and I have work tomorrow. I have been to school and to class I have given my tithe. I am gone down to Tideford to change the tracts and then the time were spent it feels as though I have not seen the reward that our land is bare of promised fruit. It seems a long while since I saw anything but desolation in this place. We have failing mines and failing communities too there are wide spaces opening up among the congregations.

I have been to the empty houses of the Lord I have seen *his* home made barren and held to ridicule the jewels that man may find in there gone to gather dust and the Book unopened though it contain such wisdom. I have known the Word of the Lord speak through me though it echoes in the emptiness with none to hear it none to listen.

Time is pressing. Twenty-seven years are gone from me at least twenty I must surely be able to remember what has passed around me. It has been so short. Yet half my life is lost and my youth is already distant I forget what it were to be a child and the forgetting is as painful as grief. What have the days amounted to? I know I have not improved the past as I ought. The sick have gone unvisited and my duties undone souls have been left unsaved and abandoned in the cold far from their Father's home. It seems as though the time were

3

never mine to govern. Have I ever been free? These years have been taken in work in earning my keep and I have no security in earthly matters nothing for myself and little enough to give to others.

I am not an uneducated man. I have received schooling and been much informed by those preachers I have had the grace to hear and by reading too. I have experienced many changes none so great as that within my own heart. I have seen some small part of this land heard men talk about many things and listened that among all the foolishness I might understand something new. But learning is passing. Seems to amount to nothing. Well what good does it serve if it will not endure what worth is it if it does not come to my aid in my work or in *his*? I confess I am worn from work I have had no good rest nor do I feel I have enough love for my duties. It seems I must always pause before fulfilling them as though to decide whether the weight were worth bearing at all.

Lately I am come to thinking on all the various agencies through which some good might be done. The tract distributor. The visitor of the sick. The Sunday School teacher. The preacher of the Gospel. All go their rounds yet we see no trophy because the poor souls they will not awaken to a sense of their danger may it please my Master to prove me wrong.

Even the Sabbath comes and they go about their work or take their rest as they please. As I walked in town today I saw a man gathering water at the well with the chapel not a hundred yards away. Oh I am certain his body thirsted enough but he ignored the deeper thirsting of his soul and the well we are offering here is more abundant than his and more refreshing too. It is a wretched state. They abuse the freedoms they have been accorded this life they have been given and they do not turn to their Lord though *he* aches for them I have felt it. They would search out their rest after hard labours yet they have no desire for the purity of peace *he* offers and content themselves with the vanity of their own mean comforts. They will lose the Sabbath and be ignorant of what they have had. Then their imaginations will fail them and they will cease to remember what it once were to have faith. They imagine they have awoken to some new world that has an easy life in store for them a place where they can rest on the Sabbath and forsake their God. But there is no new world no easy time for them and they have merely died to the old one.

I know there were better times in this country when Heaven were situated closer to earth. It were not so long ago. Even in my father's time the Church were a powerful force in this place it turned the drunk to sobriety made the profligate moral and set families right in the sight of God. I long to see *his* house renewed and made strong again.

Many times this week the fire has descended on me even in my working hours I have known the pain of the Lord as people curse and bemoan their misfortunes but come the evening they do not repair to *him* they work against themselves they do not awaken. It is said that the way of fools seems right to them. Why do they not give their hearts to God?

For our time is short. The end comes with quickening breaths. This week already has taken many with it and they go prepared or unprepared. I have seen some in this village have passed away so that children have been called to weep for parents and wives for husbands and the saying of the wise man has been renewed *Man goeth to his long home and the mourners go about the streets*. Well death is always near I do not need to be reminded of it. I feel it has been a close companion to me. I know how short life is that though in Heaven we may be granted Eternal Life on this earth our flesh is passing.

I am gone to visit the sick and saw Mr Blackmore he is weak and says he feels his Salvation is near. He is just waiting for the call. And I visited a young woman who is lain in bed these years but who keeps close to Christ and it were a joy to see that faith in someone it seems she cannot praise God enough. I think it is profitable sometimes for us to go to sickness it teaches us a lesson so that we might hear the voice of our Master calling us to be ready for *his* coming. PREPARE THYSELF *he* says I hear *his* voice it causes my soul to shake.

Yet I know I am unprepared. For my time has been wasted I have not put it to good use it has been let run through my fingers and I have been left sharp conscious of my lack of worth. Should I number my sins I have hardly the time. I do not feel within me the hope I know I should own and my labours do not bring me relief. Like the most complacent child have I tarried.

Still it is not all dark. I remain in *his* favour it seems and grateful that I am neither consumed by sickness nor bought to bow down to idols. Even as the hours of my Salvation are slipping away I am shown the mercy of *his* Grace for *he* has led me to this place and given me a knowledge of *him* in my heart and a taste of that heavenly bliss which awaits us.

So I must strive to better efforts and seize the hours left to me. I will watch my remaining days and mark them that I might see how *his* work is done. I will stake back the time make a sharp edge to catch on it as it falls and tear it out for me. I will remember those gone before I will record their names and pray for them I will keep to my stern duty. And then perhaps I shall have satisfaction and can go forth to my labours refreshed with so much cheerfulness and no aching no hard grieving no remorse of conscience no wishing that I had stayed at home.

JANUARY 1870

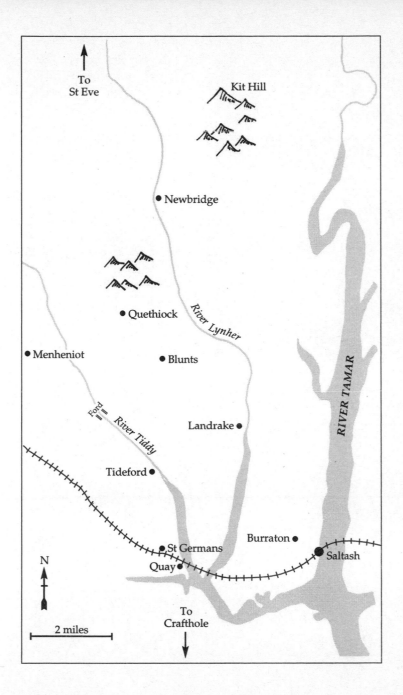

1

Well if happiness were found in a round of duties I should have had my portion today for I have not had much leisure. I am gone down early to St Germans to change the tracts they have not been done since the turn of the year. I found the workers already labouring at the quay loading the barges as the tide rose. The railway viaduct stands immense over the scene it is a remarkable construction one which seems to diminish us in comparison yet still leaves us to wonder at what men can do.

One or two of the men nodded to me as I passed by there are some here who know me. All of us wrapped thickly against the early cold I were glad I had taken an extra layer. The hawsers holding the boats were stiff with ice I have known days so cold that they have snapped robbed by the season of their taut strength the barges sliding from their position at the quay and bringing sudden shouts from the men to hold them there to fasten a new line before they drift out of reach. But the river continues to pour along regardless it has too much mud and salt for it to freeze I think or the tide is too strong and the flow too swift. Just the mill ponds at Newbridge then with a thin layer on them now though one too thin for walking or skating.

Though I have not seen it this year there is a pond on my mother's farm which often freezes. In the harder winters when I were a child my brothers and I were sent to break into it so the cattle could drink the icy water there. We took long sticks and smashed the clotted surface then carried and threw huge tiles of ice until our fingers grew numb. I remember the hard ache as they warmed so deep and persistent it seemed it would never leave.

Well this winter too has been severe there were days when I could not shake the cold no matter how hard I worked and I have felt for those who are not as strong as I am neither do they have a fire to work beside. I have not always loved the forge it is difficult labour there but the least that can be said of it is that my hands have been kept warm against the frosts. Only the tinners will have been granted similar luxury burrowed deep in the ground warmed by the heat and pressure of rock but I know how things are for them there and I do not envy them.

Still we are just a few weeks into the year and I am a little hopeful that the season is already turning. The easterlies which blew without rest all winter have lost their sharpness and kinder southern winds have swung around to us bearing with them the warmth and weight of the ocean. There is a new feel to the air a touch of cold to it still but no longer one of ice. I have thought too that the first birds are returning though it is early and perhaps my hopes run ahead of the truth of the matter. A broken flock peppered the sky today like seed thrown upwards and scattered by the winds.

I left the quayside to its industry and climbed back up the path towards St Germans. The village proper sits over the lip of the valley tucked beyond the woods a half mile from the river. It is a familiar way and pleasant to walk I have come this road many times and my thoughts tend to drift from the scenery and my particular occupation here. These steps are worn so deep into the patterned memory of my legs that I think if I were to go blind they would find their way with equal ease.

I stopped at the wayside board to post a new tract. The wooden frame supported above the verge by an upright stained with moisture. Some few patchy residues of pitch still visible but no longer enough to keep it from wear. A faint bitter smell of damp from the week's snow to the wood today though the beams drying in the day's clear air. On the wooden divider to the glass front of the board there is a tiny keyhole though there were no key that I ever knew of and the doors pull open easily enough to the touch of my fingertips. Inside just the old tract tacked there where I left it at the close of last year.

I kicked from the board the icicles which hung in a bearded row. Took a cloth to the clouded glass. Smoothed a fresh sermon sheet from the packet and fixed it there straightening the paper so that it could be clearly read then I closed the doors the swollen wood squeaking together and holding firm.

In folding the old tract down to take away with me I came to wondering how many had taken the time to stop there and profit by it. I have seen dock workers come home past it and not turn their heads. Perhaps it goes unread. That it is a sight too familiar to them so much so they no longer register it with their eyes the way we overlook much that is close to us. I have thought to mention it at the next distributors' meeting I wonder what we might do about it. Perhaps if we moved the posts made just a simple change which might encourage people to see them as though for the first time as if they were new and the Word fresh. For I have to ask myself that if it is not the means of saving souls then what good is it? May it please the Lord our God to awaken the poor souls to a sense of their danger for it is late.

I have worked during the day and in the evening I have spent my time visiting the sick it has been a rewarding duty. I have seen two widows at the almshouses Mrs Webber and Mrs Truscott but I found I had disturbed them they had been sleeping through the cold and were not keen to sit with me so I have let them be. Then Mr Blackmore briefly for he were tired his old lungs wheezing still full of dust from the ash pits and lastly Harriet French. She too were very weak her mother told me she had some pain in her chest and sides but she lay quite peaceful during my visit and did not complain of it. She is a kind girl who bears her suffering well though it has already taken her sight and I do not know how much longer she is for the world. She appears very thin with little decent meat on her but then she has survived the passing of another year full of hazards so perhaps we have reason to be hopeful.

She has a cough which scrapes like pain it stretches her face horribly when it comes and the sound of it is bitter reaching out like an infection to take hold of us. Of course we know it is a symptom of that deeper illness that has taken many away from this place and led them to desperation first. In the face of such suffering it is miracle Harr still has her faith a remarkable sight to witness but then faith is a hard stone I think quite a small thing but powerful and not easily crushed.

Some snow came as we sat and talked but it turned to rain within an hour a soft patter against the window sometimes quite hushed then renewing itself with a squall. Reminded me that there is a leak in the roof there which I have promised to help patch though it is not something I am too sure of I must find someone to ask about it.

But it were a pleasurable hour. The time glided subtly away and I felt I were called home too soon. So though I have been kept busy with no time for myself and though I do not know how to measure its gain I feel it has been a good day for my soul.

And now that today is already yesterday. I scarcely noticed how it went buried beneath the next day each erasing the last and pushing it further from our memories into oblivion. The Sabbath too has come around and were swiftly lost to us. The poor weather persisted and worsened overnight well I do not mind the rain at all but it made for a miserable walk to preach and there were a disappointing end to my walk attending. I were expecting a congregation but there were just one other there. It is a sad thought if all it takes to keep them away is a little cold and rain.

2

There were a rare day early in February when I were free from work. A day of unexpected sun when it seemed as though all would be well. The air clear and promising warm. The hope for good friendships to be resumed and my heart to be restored.

In the past I would have gone home to visit my family they live but twelve mile distant. But I am in my final weeks on trial as a local preacher and my duties have kept me busy I have determined lately to spend more time visiting those in need. I do not know how much longer they shall be with us.

Still the weather were so favourable that I stole some time early in the day to walk in the hills. When I went from home I could leave my jacket behind. The earth seemed reborn under new light. It is good land here we have green fields which make a comfortable rise and fall their hedgerows knit closely together tangled in bramble and hawthorn. The first ploughing has been done I walked through a field heavy with new soil the winter turf cut and turned. It clung to my feet they were leaden with it as I climbed the slopes.

There were a clear view to the horizon the cold air acting as a lens bringing the distant near. The scene so familiar to me all my home gathered in light and returned to my eyes. It were a comforting sensation to have everything appear close by and nothing so far away that it would seem a chore to walk it.

In the afternoon I went again to visit Harriet French and describe for her the beauty of the day. I told her how sorry I were that she were unable to share in it though I have thought since that it were perhaps not the proper thing to say that I should not distress her by glorying in just those gifts she lacks.

But at the time that thought did not come to mind she asked further how the day had been and I were stretched in recounting everything for her. Still I did not need to create anything just told her the truth of what were there.

It were like a little Heaven to be in the room with her. Harr seemed full of life and wanting to talk of many things. Of course she has no need for light in her room and I almost did not need it myself for the effect of her spirit is to brighten the room for her visitors. Her cheeks were flushed bright though the rest of her skin very pale and a hollowness to her expression. She looked so weak it seems she is waiting for the call. Yet she has peace when she lays down and when she wakes her trust is so simple and straight you would not believe she had ever known anything other than faith though she tells me that is not true. And I have wished for a long time to hear about her conversion to God to hear of some of the struggles she hints at but something always holds me back from the questions and besides she is happy to talk of simpler things and then rest a while with me waiting beside her. So I prefer not to ask no doubt the story will come to me in time. I watch her eyes flicker there are times when they move as though they saw something though it is nothing I can follow.

We have seen many made blind from birth whose eyes are sheet white like Paul their eyeballs coated with scales. I wonder what it would be like to see nothing but a milky screen keeping you apart from the world. They say our souls are known only unto the Lord and remain a mystery to us but I have often thought that *he* grants us more knowledge of them than we are commonly told. We may see the evidence of the people we are in our eyes and it is not by accident that we call them *windows to the soul*. I have learned to look for truth there for it looks to God and it reflects *his* Glory. So it has lately occurred to me that perhaps those who have grown blind and lost their sense of the world have their souls stolen from them too removed from their eye sockets and exchanged for smooth white marbles. That something of their humanity is

16

taken that they are made half-man or woman that the loss of the world is also the loss of something within them. Or perhaps their souls are trapped inside known only to God sheared from this world their ties scraped thin by a knife and snapped. I have been a little disturbed by the thought of it.

Harr though has been spared that. Well her sight is lost but her soul has been saved and we are free to behold it. Her eyes glisten like pebbles beneath a clear stream. Around the pupils there is grey but they reflect like a fine fabric the light of the room and take on other colours I have seen them blue or green or yellow according to the hour and the colour of her dress or if sunlight shone in through the window.

Once when I sat with her mother I found myself distracted by a sweet scent come from somewhere in the house an odour I knew but could not place. I went from room to room passing from the kitchen up the stairs to visit the girl still puzzled by the sweetness and I did not know that there were a burst of irises on her dresser until I saw the sea-blue reflected in her eyes.

I know Harr relinquished her sight slowly it would seem a terrible thing to lose the beauty of *his* world in this way. Yet she has never complained to me she seems surprised when I ask her and says she can remember perfectly how things around her appeared when she were young and that she does not need to see them any longer.

They might not be so beautiful as I remember she says and laughs.

She says it were a long summer sunset as the light died a wonderful thing. That there were gold before the dark. I think how brave she is. And as her blindness is invisible to us I imagine that some visitors if they came would not know it at all for she knows her room well and her hearing is quite acute there is something of an illusion she creates to set guests at their ease.

Sister French I say when I knock on the wood of the door-frame.

And she knows it is me because she has heard my voice downstairs but if she is not too tired she is always pleased for visitors and answers with pleasure and surprise in her voice Brother Wenmoth she says and asks me in.

If she stays awake and desires it I read to her. She has a book of poems given by a friend but I have trouble with it and am embarrassed to say the words wrong. Well I have no facility for the rhythm of it and the language seems fanciful to me. Sometimes she would correct me and I would try the passage again but it has never come easily. Other times I see her make as though to tell me I have made a mistake but then in an act of sympathy change her mind and allow me to continue. Either way I am left feeling uncomfortable. And then among the poems there are several in praise of Nature but the verses seem to me false and overly refined everything that Nature is not. I do not have a liking for it. The rhyming lines might as well be hymns without music and are less substantial fare for it. Though they call the land *divine* they seldom mention our Lord.

So I take the Bible and we read the stories there. I am much relieved that we have fallen into this pattern I have a great preference for this and feel there is much to be learned from hearing the old stories again more riches than in any poetry.

Today when I visited we talked of the life at Church and she seemed sad she could not be part of it.

You must miss the fellowship I said.

It is the singing I miss more she confessed.

She smiled as she said it her smile is a vital and curious thing to see for it is undirected to any part of the room in particular and entirely unconscious of itself there is no affectation to it.

I offered her we could sing there but she laughed and said she did not have the energy and perhaps it were not proper. I thought there were nothing improper about praising God but she were tired and happy so I did not say so I understood that she were unwilling to disturb her mother and I did not wish us to spend our time here worried would her mother hear would her mother come up.

So she talked a while about her memories of Church from when she were a child and her memories were so warm they caused me to think much on my own childhood I record here some of what she said.

She were perhaps nine year old the time she spoke of. On Sundays her mother would send her and William down to fix the shutters in her aunt's shop and bolt the door top and bottom. At a quarter to eleven she went with them to the little Methodist chapel at the top of the hill she spoke of summers when the grass were tall and being forbidden from play for fear of spoiling her dress. Her aunt wore a stiff silk frock with an embroidered front she remembers it exactly her hands trace the design in the air for me. In those days more people from the village attended. How sad it is no longer true. Even in these few short years the size of the congregation has lessened and I often imagine how it were in my grandfather's time when the Church saw a great revival I think it must have been as it says in the Bible when the stones of the street cried out that the rocks of the churches were full of praise. There were a marvellous effusion of the Holy Spirit. Come the Sabbath people came to hear the preachers they gathered in their hundreds in many places over by Gwennap Pit or in this circuit out in the open on the green beside the chapel.

I wondered with Harr how it might have been but she does not know those times any more than I do.

Now not even this family attends though it is circumstances which keep them from it. Since Harr is homebound her mother is become a Quaker and meets in the village not with us at the chapel. And so they are left off the Church rota of sick well I have made efforts to change that situation I do not think that we are intended to care solely for our own.

I imagine her now sitting on the pews much as she sits when we bring her downstairs her ears bent to listen to the sermon. Perhaps she did as I and my brothers did when our eyes wandered to play in the whorl of the wood in front of us and we would imagine that small worlds were birthed there full of stories for us. Or perhaps she leant back to follow the arch of the stone supports and wonder how all this had been done for our Lord. It were clear from her memories that the loss she feels is not a privation of communion with the Lord for she has that here her spirit is open but for the chapel itself the stone building she knew and the people who inhabited it.

If she and William were good during the sermon she says they were sometimes given a sweet to suck on the way home. And if the weather were fine they were permitted to change from their clothes and afterwards play in the sloping garden at the back of her aunt's house but they knew not to shout or be noisy on the Sabbath.

At the bottom of the garden there were a running brook where they played she smiled as she remembered it. They tapped the stones to bring out eels from under them. She said how strange they looked so long and wriggling. I remarked on the wonder of them how that although they lived underwater I have heard it said they travel distances as great as those of men.

She spoke with clear happiness but I were disturbed by it because she talked of times that were already long gone and she would have no other life on this earth save a few more months of suffering. But she does not count the past as lost. I wonder if she knows it will not return. That the old lives will not be lived again that we stumble to our end along new roads through shortening days.

Our talk had left her tired and her eyes filling with water. But her smile were still bright so I knew that these memories were precious and we had not done wrong in retelling them. And as though in compensation for that happiness I felt a drawing sadness when it came time for me to leave. On my way out I left 2d. with Mrs French implied that it were from the chapel though it came from my own pocket. And though it were not much I have needed to be careful in my expenditure for the remainder of the week.

I walked home. There were a fine sunset. A thin strip of sky above the horizon took on the light of gold then turned fiery and blazed away until it burned to ash just grey cloud left like smoke after it.

3

This last year of work has been made bearable by my visits to Harriet French and her family and of the moments of pleasure I have lately been afforded so many were in her company. Her room offers an unusual rest a place by the wayside which has often been waiting for me. Her soul seems so blessed with our Master's love that to be in her presence feels to bring me closer to *him*. She may have gone into sickness but the reward for her is that she has been saved and her company lightens my burden and eases the struggles of my soul. She breaks the days.

She lives with her mother and brother in a small house in one of the poor streets of St Germans. I am acquainted with them through my mother she knew them when Harr's aunt owned a shop in the neighbouring village and I understand there is some relationship on that side of the family though it has never been traced for me. It is distant enough to be forgotten. Of course the shop now is shut and her aunt's house sold the father's death and Harr's illness have brought them into difficult circumstances.

And there are many families here with similar troubles so I am often come to St Germans to visit the sick it seems there is no shortage of work for the Church in this place. *For the poor always ye have with you* we are told and it seems a sad truth though I wonder if it is necessary. Sometimes I am riled when I walk past the estate and see the wealth evident behind the walls. The Squire is an upright man a Christian I do not judge him to be unkind for he cares for his tenants well and does not cast them from their houses if they cannot pay rent but he is a rich man all the same and I think his money might do some good in this parish if it were shared more evenly.

My approach to the village takes me by the estate gardens. And it is a curious thing because I look at the place to judge the wealth of it but the sight of those wide lawns provokes in me an odd nostalgia for the place perhaps for a life I have not lived but were always strangely desirous of.

A short walk away the houses of the poor are in bad repair and there is rubble spreading by the sides of the road. I am reminded of my own blessings. The children who play in the street are in old clothes almost worn through and dirty but they have nothing better I am thankful I were never reduced to that state. On my last visit I saw a boy without shoes his feet blackened by dirt and no doubt blood cut on sharp rocks but still running away around the corner when he saw me. And then I saw him again when I came round the corner hugging his mother's thigh and circling round behind her skirts.

The houses were once whitewashed but the coating is greatly decayed become cracked and grimy. There is refuse heaped in piles hard by the walls and one or two houses I am unhappy to visit the stench is so bad as it rises foetid and rotten from puddles. It is no wonder sickness lingers in these places.

These villages were smaller once and the area reliant on its farms I cannot help but think that those were happier days. For the land has been opened up with mines and quarries and many men come to work in the ground extracting the wealth from it. Yet for all the injury it has inflicted upon the earth and the changes it has wrought on these communities it does not seem to have brought riches for them. There is no family in this street that has escaped hard times many sons and daughters have been taken from them I think I could have a full quota of labour in a short space yet often enough I have time only for Mrs French and her children. She had no other family except her husband and a sister and both were carried from her before she had children able to support her and now her daughter too has been taken sick.

The widow's house is among the smaller buildings here. Tall chestnuts rise bare-armed behind the row their interest turned from the sky to the ground their roots searching for life deep in the earth. The home is merely a cottage built on the slant of the hill so the upper floor is longer than the one beneath it. Just a kitchen down below and at the front a small porch roofed with broken slate. Not quite straight on the roof is a stone-piled chimney stack one of the pots broken off and shorter than the other.

They have two bedrooms above of course one is now used as a small infirmary and Harr's brother William is moved into his mother's room. William is much younger than Harr and I know him a little he attends the Sunday School in my class though his appearance is an irregular thing. He often comes to linger by the door during my visits but he will not interrupt us. I notice him arrive but then become absorbed in talking with Harr and when I leave he has disappeared and I did not see him go. Well I am sure he does not resent the attention his sister receives she is terrible sick and in need of our time and prayers. This home is ruled by disease its lives given over to care for the dying. But how else can it be?

The aspect of the place would seem unwelcoming then it is a poor house and cold. But I have experienced many pleasurable moments in this place and I am warmed by the sight of it my step up towards the door is optimistic and light. For it is a valuable thing I feel in those minutes hearing Mrs French move across the kitchen and anticipating her voice she will invite me in and I can spend a short time with her until the moment is right for me to say well I shall see how she is and then I can leave her and go upstairs where I will find that Heaven awaiting me.

4

Despite the pleasure of those visits my life this last year has been hard for me in certain respects. I have been sharp aware that I were allowed little chance to see my old friends and family. I have beloved friends in the Church too but since I am come to Quethiock I see them much less they have stayed in their home circuit at St Eve. The Bible Class at St Germans is ill attended I have not found much fellowship. And this year too is moving along rapidly we are already into its second month and I have felt quite low because it seemed that it would be another year in which I would lack for company. So I were much delighted to have received some unexpected good cheer this week the news that Brother Tripp my old classmate James has returned for a while to this parish he has come on the train from Penzance. I saw his father in the street and he had the news for me I confess it has been a frustrating week because I have not been able to concentrate my mind on present tasks for my excitement at seeing him the following Sabbath.

I were due to preach that day under my sponsor Mr Roberts so I asked Mr Tripp to pass on a message that I would be glad to see James at the service. I saw him coming up the path as I waited in the vestry greeting the congregation. His gait so familiar that I recognized the movement long before his face had come into focus. I suppose that having known friends for so long we remain attuned to such impressions whatever the years that have separated us. His rolling lope feet tending outwards as though he were slightly bowlegged from years on a horse although I do not think he has ridden much.

Brother Wenmoth he said and we embraced.

I'm glad you came I said and I could not have felt it more.

Then we went in and gave our praise and it were a refreshing time. I felt I rushed the sermon to sooner speak with James afterwards so the service were a little swiftly done but I do not think my enthusiasm were misplaced. Mr Roberts were the first to speak to me after the service.

I can only trust you have a good dinner waiting for you he said dryly. He leant forward to my ear. A little rushed today he said but he put his hand on my shoulder before he went an affirmation that he were pleased enough.

I stood by the door to bless the congregation as they departed for their homes James lingered at the back until the people had gone and we could talk.

And how are you surviving? he asked me.

I said well I thought and we exchanged our news.

He has been in the West these last years a long way down beyond even Penzance and he provided me a good account of the work of the Church there. I were brought to remember the hard time Wesley had in converting that place and thought it good that his work endured.

He has found employment as a labourer and a position as a steward in the chapel there. I told him I had an apprenticeship with the smith and he were surprised at the turn in my fortunes.

But you are a farmer Charles he said he were teasing me I thought.

Well no longer I said.

And how is it?

Hard I said. The hours are long and exhausting with not much to show for them.

He nodded. Well we are instructed not to worry about providing for ourselves he said.

And that is true but his saying it made me wonder if he in fact were free not to worry about his circumstances I knew that I were not.

And are you back now? I asked.

No not for long he said and the answer were a disappointment to me. My sister is ill so I have come back for her but I need to return to work and I have other matters left behind me too.

I told him I were sorry for his sister but he said that things were well that they were in the Lord's hands and he were quite confident she would be saved. And he rushed past the subject full of energy for talking so we came to be speaking of brighter things. He asked after my family he knew my mother and brothers well and I gave him what news I had though it were old news not refreshed since Christmas.

I found him pleasingly unchanged in his energies though grown up as we all are. The edge of wildness taken off him a little. We stood cold in the yard of the chapel and caught up on our stories. Our conversation were much interrupted by the noise of a group of boys playing in the field having been released from their class. Their shouts too loud for the Sabbath. James has his old ease to him and he were not distracted just smiling from time to time as the sounds returned with increasing vigour. But I were more bothered by the disturbance for it were no mere working day and it did not seem an appropriate way to pass solemn hours. So half of me scorned the lads for it because they had no sense of their duties. Delight in their hearts plenty but none of it directed towards the Lord they had not assumed their responsibilities for the Sabbath. And then half of me envied them their freedom for having now what I had once and would dearly love again.

The Sabbath was made for man James said when we spoke of it and I were reminded that we are encouraged to be like the children to turn our minds to curiosity and wonder when we consider our Lord.

And in truth it were good to see them playing together the timing of it were quite propitious because it reminded us both of our own youths not so far into the past only a few seasons but feeling far away and it were pleasant to revive the memories.

We played together and that is an unusual thing for me because I have four brothers sufficient company to consume any child's youth. I think that James were the only good friend I had outside my family and he were my age too so we were schooled together and grew up likewise so we have come from the same root. We played together as though we would be children always we were free to run in the woods creating great adventures for ourselves.

Though it is a strange thing because now that I have come to revive those days in my mind I remember that there were another friend we spent time with. Someone I have not thought of for many years. A girl who lived at Newbridge not far from James's cottage and close enough to our farm. Her name escapes me I cannot recall it. The three of us met at the mill pool near her house. We picked blackberries from the hedges along the lanes and spoiled our appetites with their sweetness collecting the remainder for her mother's kitchen. How strange to suddenly remember these images and yet still not know the name. It cannot be so long ago.

Those days must mean something but I do not understand what and I am left to doubt the worth of my memories for they cannot bring back the happiness and every delight I have in them seems but a form of sadness and loss. They were glad days and I do not own them any longer. And then I wonder too how many such days there truly were fewer perhaps than I seem to remember but they burrow so deep.

I waited with James a long time after the service until we were the only two remaining standing outside the church the steward having closed the doors beside us and gone away wishing us a good morning. This time with my old friend seemed very precious but I knew it were soon ended that we must both face our duties in the remainder of the day.

I have my trial soon I said. Will you come?

He said it were excellent news but it transpired that the date fell badly for him and he could not come that day he would be visiting with his family and I were disappointed by that. But he assured me we would spend some time together soon and his grin were cheering and familiar just completely without weight as easy as a child's and reminded me strongly of the boy he had been. I thought then that perhaps our pasts were not yet done with that we possessed something of them still. We walked down the lane together until our ways parted and I watched him go.

5

James's visit has left me in good cheer but it has been a struggle to keep my spirits up since. February has been cold and miserable and the weather is threatening to continue the same. I have worked long hours in the forge and been sore from work this week so I had not looked forward to the Sabbath as I should. Though I am ashamed to say it the truth is that I would rather have had some rest. I have had duties at chapel and the Sunday School and then there were the visiting so the day has been as many other days already gone by.

Quethiock chapel is closed these years so I go down to St Germans to teach. It means a long walk but it is not an unpleasant duty I have enjoyed schooling the children and remember how much I profited from instruction in the Lord when I were young. It has often been a revelation for me that while I have been reading the Bible for study I come across a story familiar to me from my classes at St Eve and which the intervening years had threatened to take from me. *His* Word can sit deep inside us and profit us though we do not think of it. I find these stories powerful things invaluable in themselves and we have much to learn from our encounters with them.

The school here is smaller than the one I attended if you were to count just my brothers and me we had almost as many as I have now. I know many of the families here are farmers and must work on the Sabbath but they have duties here too and all their labours will not profit them if they do not look to the source of their blessing.

And I must ask myself how many of those who come to school will go on to accept their Saviour in their hearts. For this is the way of things young people are deserting the Lord abandoning their search for the pearl of great price and satisfying themselves with worldly ambitions. There were only six schoolers today. Three from the village two of the young Tamblyns from Pencorme Farm. The boys in their caps and the girls in wide-skirted crinoline and their best white aprons down to their ankles they hardly know their catechisms and respond dumbly to almost every question I ask of them. They do not seem to have much sense of what they are doing here. William French were there he wants for Christian instruction far more than his sister. It were not long after he were born that his father were taken from him lost to an accident at the mine face. Well I know what it is to have lost a father when young so I have had sympathy for him that were a sad time for me. And though Mrs French is no longer with our chapel she sends William along here and I think she is right in wanting him schooled.

He is a likeable child but causes me some sorrow. For though he has never given me cause for trouble I know he does not enjoy school. There are his absences and then even when he is in attendance he never raises his hand in response to my questions on our stories yet when I call his name he knows the answers well enough. But it is as though the answer means nothing to him his manner is dispassionate and cold. He is like to spend his time looking out the schoolroom window through the one clear pane that has been spared staining well I have half a mind to laugh it off because there are enough days when I too would much rather be outside but there is a darkness to his mood that makes me think he is not looking to go out for play with friends or take joy in the day but take himself away from the world for a while. But I like the boy well. I remember how it were when I were a child I had no great love for school and no love for God though it were unthinkable that I would not go. He has had a hard life too and his mother cannot always afford the class fees so there is no blame in it. He has none of the joy in childhood it is a sad thing because he will grow old soon enough and have no sweet memories to temper the hardness of living. His circumstances have lent him eyes guarded with a knowledge of suffering which I feel he is too young for.

Still I trust that God has a purpose in it and although he comes only to please his mother I know that if he and I persist we might make some progress and I have hope that my Master will look after him.

We read together the Gospel of Luke 21st Chapter the story of the widow who gave just two mites to the treasury but were loved by the Lord better than the rich man. I thought because the families here were poor they might get comfort from it I wanted them to see the purpose of this story but there were little interest.

And why were she loved more? I asked them.

But they were quiet their eyes cast down. I let them think on it a while but there were nothing forthcoming I wish I saw a little more effort from them.

Come now I said. Do you think it is better to give less to the church?

And I saw that had confused them a little.

William I said knowing he would speak if I asked him and hoping it might encourage his classmates.

Because there were nothing she didn't give he said. Because she didn't keep anything for herself.

And the hurt in his voice reminded me his mother is a widow and so perhaps the story were not so wisely chosen after all so Yes I said Yes that is right and then we left it aside.

I had them copy out some Bible verses I chose 23rd Psalm *The Lord is my shepherd I shall not want* thinking they would like it and hoping they would remember the lines. Their writing is not so good the youngest Tamblyn girl cannot really form her letters at all but they will not learn a thing if they do not have the chance to practise so I do not think it does any harm. I do not have much grammar to instruct them with but my handwriting is passable I can demonstrate how it should be and it is better than nothing at all. For writing we have square slates framed in wood so the children can hold them cleanly. And though the slates wipe clean at the end of class the effect of many Sabbaths' work is a chalky residue so that the once black slates are clouded and the writing on them always a little duller than previously.

The end of our hour arrived quickly and the chapel emptied out I let the children go and instructed them to read some of the Bible when they could. William were first to the door but I called him and held him back a moment after the others had gone.

How is your sister? I asked. Should I come by and visit?

He considered this a moment and I waited long breaths before he answered.

I am not going straight home he said. I have errands to run.

Well I did not know whether to believe him it were the Sabbath and not a day when errands were run. But it hardly mattered because if he were not going straight home it removed my excuse to visit and perhaps it would be an imposition on his family so I resolved to spend some time alone that night in prayer for them. I thanked him for his work and asked him to send my regards to Harriet and his mother. And then he were gone slipped out and disappeared he is a slight thing quick on his feet but not much build to him at all which made me concerned that they did not have enough to eat. I will consider the matter and perhaps there is something that can be done.

I were much amused after school. A woman waited for me I thought she had come to thank me for my labours but no she had come to see me to ask what she should do with her son's attendance tickets which he had from us. The children collect them to exchange for prayer books or gospels at the end of each year. And she expected a reward even though he left our class a long time ago to attend the parish Sunday School in the village. She were very insistent she made as though she would argue loudly with me but I did not have the will for it she said she would like to see fair play that she only wanted what is right. And this is what amused me. That she should come to a Sunday School teacher who has given up his time to try and instruct her children in the right ways and that she should demand something from him. So I thought where is the Father going to have *his* fair play from?

6

Well it has been four years since the blessed meeting when I felt the knowledge of God warm my breast and two since the Word came that I should preach. And on this last Sabbath my time on trial is ended and I have been welcomed into the service of the Church as my father were before me and his father too before him. I have spent eighteen months under the tutelage of Mr Roberts I helped him in his services for long weeks before I had the opportunity to speak the Word on my own and while it has been a frustrating time with my heart longing to preach he were a thoughtful instructor and it were a profitable means of grace.

The walk were eight miles each way sixteen together it passed pleasantly away. I arose by half past five for the journey and came in good time to Tideford for my duties then on to St Germans for the local preachers' meeting and to make my trial. There were a real frost to the morning air and when the light came it were pale and yellow the beginnings of a bright clear day. We are barely come into March and must still wait a while for the first evidence of colour in the trees the green budding of new leaves but I sensed it were not so far away that the woods are stirring again preparing for the year. The birds were more numerous too and very loud.

The fellowship were strong a large number had come for the meeting it were a restorative sight. I saw my Godfather Mr Pendray among them. We warmed ourselves with the opening hymn sang full rousing choruses and I felt the spirit to be very much alive. We sang Wesley's great hymn *My Jesus to know And feel his blood flow 'Tis life everlasting 'Tis Heaven below* and all our blood flowed a little stronger after that.

Felt it a dry time then to listen to Mr Roberts I heard his sermon from Proverbs 18th Chapter *The name of the Lord is a strong tower.* What he preached were the Truth his words fell right but I seemed to need to listen hard to feel much refreshed by it. Perhaps my mind were too preoccupied with my own sermon that day. He led the Bible Class following the sermon and it were a profitable use of time. The number that stayed on meant we were decently sized there were a few men of the circuit I knew Brother Cottle Brother Hawke Mr Verran and his wife as well as some others I had not met. I were most grateful for my Godfather to be there he were not obliged to come and must have caught the early train from Saltash to be with us.

Though he lives some way distant now I have known Mr Pendray my whole life he were a friend of my father for many years in their youths they worked together in the mines. From my earliest memories he were a regular visitor to our farm and an uncle to me though in truth no relation. Well I lost my own father before I were twelve years old he had endured illness a long time and were released from his suffering.

Mr Pendray has no family of his own though I understand from my mother that there were an elder brother who died but I did not meet him and do not know if he were taken long ago. So we were something of a surrogate home for him. He were made my Godfather when I were born and is Godfather to two of my brothers also with me being the youngest of our lot. I have often been brought to wondering on the kindnesses he made towards us he has conducted himself with more than the duty of his role. I have come to know a little of his own past how he has dedicated his life to the Church and become a fine example to us would that I had his devotion. But he has told me that there were a time in his youth when he lived a sinful life he gave his hours to drink and blasphemy and were almost destroyed by it. To watch him now it is hard to believe it. He has none of the wildness in his eyes that possesses a man who drinks he stands straight in the sight of the Lord. He were an ugly thing then he says well perhaps it is true I have known drink maim men's spirits and twist their bodies accordingly. But it seems time has found his features to be yielding and shaped them with kindness it has taken his beaked skull and smoothed it with the elegance of a seabird's his bald forehead stretching back. His eyes sit deep in his face as though they had seen too much of the world and retreated from it in deference or patience. His face is softened and kind framed by silver thick whiskers his large hands tremble but are gentle in their actions. His black suit is brushed and tidy the waistcoat and jacket buttoned tightly to the top a white preacher's tie folded in a neat loose knot. There is a solid presence to him though he is slower now with age. I have always been happy for his company there is comfort in it.

I know how he came to Christ almost a generation back when he were younger than I am now he has told me of the effect it had of hearing a great preacher one Martin Bright speak to him and how it inspired him. The name is familiar to me I heard my father talk of him many times. Back then Mr Pendray worked in the mine with my father this were before he were saved and he spent his money on sin and found his way too often to the alehouse to squander all that he had earned. And one time that preacher came to the door of the alehouse which were a brave thing to do for you could be drenched in beer before you spoke but this occasion were different he declared every man in that black hole damned unless they came out from under the Devil's sway that they would see their families made bankrupt and starving their souls burning in Hell. And one or two of them stopped to listen Mr Pendray said he were greatly affected by the lesson something within him responding to the Word and he resolved in himself to no longer waste his days but look for happiness in the Lord. Well it were a different conversion to my own it required great outward change on his part but he were healed in time and forgiven his sins.

The following day he worked in the mine and all day were singing praises to his Lord and giving thanks that he had been saved exhorting his fellow tinners to do the same. His heart were roaring he has told me and it did not seem right if he did not roar too. So my father heard and went along to pray with him and welcome him to the Christian fold and they became close friends after that and would attend class together even after my father left the mine and went away to marry.

This Martin Bright took much time to talk to my Godfather and instruct him in the changes in his life and he has not forgotten the kindnesses that were afforded to him then so perhaps he has sought to repay some of them in me. Or else my Godfather misses his friend my father and I am come to assume that role though I am not him.

Your father would have been glad to see today he said when we gathered after the service.

And I were pleased he had mentioned him.

His legs tire from standing too much so we sat together in the hall and discussed the sermon I think he too had found it dry. His tastes were always for those who spoke the Word with passion for a loud voice and strong message. It has been a wonder to me he has not run off to join the Bible Christians and gone to sing and dance with them. But then he were always loyal to his Mother Church and has calmed down a little now with age so perhaps he has no desire to be running anywhere.

I asked him how his journey had been and if he were not too tired from it but his answer were very cheerful and he seemed well.

We talked more about the Word as it had been given then he came to ask after my family but I thought he might have seen them more recently than I because I have not been home since Christmas. But he had not travelled out for several weeks neither and were disappointed not to have more news from me.

Before we rejoined the others he bent forward to put his hand on my head and made a prayer that I would be blessed and might fulfil with honour my future duties. It were a kind gesture I felt my Master's presence with us.

While the afternoon were still fresh outside and the sun bright a few of us gathered together for a short walk through the village. It were sad to see how many people we passed who were not dressed for chapel nor for Church either. But they would not meet my eyes nor greet our party from the chapel it is true that they feel the effect of their transgressions in their hearts they are not so hidden from them as many think. Well we shall give them time to see if they are able to do something about this and we shall hope it is not too late for them. Salvation is promised to each of us and we must improve ourselves if we are to attain it.

We had simple fare with members of the parish and Mr Roberts gave our offering of thanks then prayed for me that I might be accepted by God and the circuit as a worthy disciple. I blessed the Lord that by *his* Grace he has kept me these years and not allowed me to stray from *his* path. And we passed some more time in talk and prayer it were soon the hour for our service.

I felt the Lord with me for my trial. Last night I read Wesley's sermon on the new birth and feel I am growing in Christ. I have been thinking how rapid time flees and that I must hold on to this time and walk with my Master before it slips away. I remember the lessons my father gave on speaking the Word and the great humility come upon him who presumes to have it on his lips. In the steps before the pulpit I bowed my head and gave one prayer at each step it is a habit I have developed which makes for a slow ascent certainly but I find the extra seconds quite valuable in preparing my mind. At the first I remembered my father and through him my family and friends. Then I thought of the poor and sick those who need the blessing of God. The next step I gave thanks for my Saviour Jesus Christ that *he* died for my sins then with the final pace I prayed the Word of God be with me and I stepped forward made my greeting and spoke from the Bible. I felt my father would have been pleased.

We sang our opening hymn and I thought how few the voices were in the chapel and many of them had come only for today that most weeks the congregation would be thinner still. And because I were rich that day in the love of God I felt angry that there were so few of us gathered here and so little love for the Lord among *his* people. I thought it were a fleeting thing but this anger did not pass away it took me right over a strange feeling in my shoulders and arms. I would have reproached myself for it or sought to wrestle myself free but it did not feel like the anger were my own and I had no control over it. There were a pain in my front like a good knife pressed sharp to my chest and a lump at the back of my throat pushing to speak my collar were tight beneath my chin I were sure my face were quite red with the constriction. I let the last line of the hymn stay unsung and took deep breaths.

And then when the lessons had been read and we had finished praising God a second time I tried to speak my introduction to the scripture *Except ye see sights and wonders ye will not believe* but I choked with the passage leaping in me flaring with warmth and do not know if it got out right. Then my notes fell aside for I felt words come from my stomach they were hot in my throat and blazed in my mouth and I spoke through it until the light had burned white and faded again and the time were spent. I preached the Word on Thomas from the Gospel of John 20th Chapter 24th Verse for the attendance here tells me the state of the Church. I know how doubt and disbelief have come upon many people who were once with us and they do not turn around.

7

I experienced a rare exhilaration when we were done and had great energy for the walk home. The night sky were blissful clear and full of stars so many of them they hid the familiar constellations among the busy bright. So although there were a shorter path home I chose the longer route for it enabled me to spend more time outside the extra hour were surely not wasted. It were chilly around my ears so I wrapped my scarf right round my head and put my hat on top it must have looked quite strange but I did not mind too much who saw me. My heart were joyful and I were consequently not so worried about my appearance. I took the way north up along the river to Tideford and then the empty lanes home to Quethiock coming in by the church.

It seemed a perfect day spent with the Lord and *his* congregation. But always my lightness of feeling passes swiftly away when I come close to my lodgings and the beauty of the evening which had allowed me to forget my worries seemed to slip from me. It is a pleasant enough cottage. An old maid's house built at the foot of a larger home though the two are now divided by a new wall and burgeoning hedge. Built of uneven walls of seamed Cornish stone and thick slate bound by rough mortar a climber making its beginnings up the side. Most of the year there are flowers in the garden on either side the path we have crocuses and daffodils in spring and richly coloured chrysanthemums to follow. The low front door which were not built for someone of my frame I have to stoop through it. It looks a cosy home but seeing it always brings my heart to frown because of my circumstances here just to think of them makes my mind troubled and heavy it drags my soul to earth.

I came in quiet to avoid disturbing my landlady. She sleeps early it is sad she misses so much of an evening such as we have had. Left my shoes in the small porch and stood there a moment to listen if she were about but everything were still. In the kitchen the range were cold she had not thought to leave it burning for me so I could heat some broth. Well I have been given no reason to expect luxury here but it felt like a mean omission. There were no food prepared for me neither well by rights I should have had a meal today but I felt I had eaten enough in the day so I went again alone into my room. It is a small place with just a thin rope-strung bed which is too short for me though I have learned to accustom myself to its length. There is a little window but it faces north the wrong way and I do not get much sunlight. Still if I put my head up to it I can see the field and the tall elms at the far end and in the summer I can sleep with it open and let the fresh air in to help me rest.

My situation in these lodgings is uncomfortable. I feel my landlady does not want me to be certain of my position here and I know I have been suffered in her house solely on the good word of others sponsors from the Church who have spoken up for my character. I am sure she would prefer to find someone of more respectable income but lodgings are not in such great demand and anyone who had the right money to spend would surely stay somewhere grander. But because she has no proper income and must owe her own rent to the estate she takes what she can. Still I am not made to feel welcome. Almost every shilling I earn finds its way to her in some form for rent or food and it makes me angry that I work so hard only to see her profit by it. Well I do not have much choice in the arrangement but I wish it were soon over.

I have her son's room one Richard Grose I never knew him I understand he is some years younger than me. He is married though and gone to Australia. Well she had just one son who survived because her husband died early of sickness and now he is far away so perhaps it is no surprise she is bitter with abandonment and perhaps some of the blame handed my way comes because I am not him. He sends her letters and she preaches to me from them she tells me how her Richard is now earning a fair fortune how he is becoming an important man and how her Richard is married or how she has a new grandchild. And I must hold my tongue or find something to occupy my hands because I want to ask her if she is so pleased with her son then why does she complain that he went or why does she not go to him. And I wonder if the letters contain quite what she says because if her Richard were indeed doing so well surely she would see some of it. I am not ignorant of these things I have a brother gone to Australia for some seven years he has a family there and I know that things do not come easily for him and the work is hard.

But I should not judge I am not perfect in this matter I love my family dear but cannot get home to visit them often neither do I have much money to send them and they live a fair amount closer to me than Mrs Grose does to her Richard.

It is a tiresome situation. I do right by my duties but she finds fault in everything I do there is always some chore she finds for me some task she feels has not been done well enough and she berates me as though I had no other labour to go to. If I am late from the chapel she will not keep food for me she makes no allowance for my involvement in my Master's work. Each week too she doubts my payment though I have always made it promptly and have never been in debt to her. I think if she were truly happy with her son she would not treat me so poorly.

She does not understand why a man in my position is still working and serving debts of time and training how I can be respectable if I have reached my age without a family or the means to support them. But I have worked hard my whole life I spent long years on the farm until it did not profit us for me to work there more and then I were called away and found an apprenticeship.

43

No she would have more love for me if she had happiness in herself but all she wants from me is my earnings she does not care to have friends I think she brings her loneliness on herself. It is sad to see for while she clings to money as her means of salvation her care for the Lord lessens. Oh I know she mixes with the Catholics and I do not judge her for seeking company but I cannot help think that she does not feel the love of God in her heart. I think she would greatly profit from a true Church that might bring her closer to God.

She has no time for prayer before meals and were offended by my suggestion that we do so. I pause and offer thanks in silence. I have no heart for argument with her I have a strong dislike for quarrelling for my blood being raised by words. Anger renders us foolish and I hate to feel it. It causes an unpleasant feeling in me worse than being struck it makes me feel very ashamed.

Well it had been a glorious day but I felt my heart were being clouded with these thoughts and that they might overly shadow my blessings so I have done my best to cast them from my mind and meditate on better things.

I lit the candle stub in my room then knelt down beside my bed to pray still fresh from my new baptism in the Church and remembered my father he would have been glad to have seen today.

8

My father were a righteous man. He were called from the mines he had no education and no easy life but he were eloquent in the witness of Christ. There is language come from a heart open to God that the mind cannot know. I saw how he preached and became lost in the words and afterwards did not know a thing of what he had said just his heart strangely warmed. Well I have felt a little of it myself tonight but I wish it were less rare. A rapture we could touch on in our daily lives something divine we might experience and it not be a mystery to us.

He knew a great deal of suffering his body were broken by work. First the mines before God called him from that danger and brought him to my mother and the farm. But the damage were mostly done and long after he had come out from underground there were dark grit inside him still and sharp pain when it passed in his water. There were times when that pain grew great in his back and sides and crippled him he were not fit for work seemed a broken man looked after by my mother unable to perform his labours. But he said not one word in complaint and his quietness were one of wisdom and forbearance. He had no side of foolishness to him. Well there were men that called him weak said that he were half a man and no use for this life so that more than once I were made to feel ashamed for him but he were a good father a sober man and I think that many of those who mocked him would be richer if they had but a small part of his grace.

I saw too on the Sabbath when he were planned to preach and that strange strength came upon him. Because he were weak he clutched the rails on either side the pulpit and anchored himself there the white of his knuckled fists evident against the varnished wood. He stayed this way the whole service and would not loosen his grip till his sermon were ended and the last hymn sung and he could collapse exhausted in his chair. The remainder of those days he would sit at his desk grey-faced and weary and we were not to disturb him. If he took food I would bring it to him there and sometimes find him asleep slumped over the desk. I remember once his pain were so severe that he were holding his head in his hands and weeping. I turned away and took the food back to my mother and did not know what to say to her so deeply were I shaken by the sight. We do not expect to see our parents this way we cannot see such things and remain innocent.

Perhaps the Devil tested him with these afflictions but his faith were always strong. His knowledge of his Master fulfilled him. When he sang his voice owned a health his body did not have it were powerful and clear and resounded with conviction. And it were these things more than any sermon I ever heard that provided me a demonstration of the work of God in this parish and made me thirst for the mystery of Christ though I were too young to properly know it. My father then were long gone when I finally took Christ into my heart but I am grateful to him for preparing the way.

I have too few memories of him. How he taught me to pray by clasping his hands around mine pressing them tightly and sounding the words with me I still think of it when I knot my hands together. Over dinner he would speak at length of the meetings he had attended and the preachers he had heard and we were to sit and listen and profit by it. He were a great talker. If guests came by while he were sick they would often get his interest up and they would stay long hours with the Bible and argue loudly. Sometimes I awoke in the night thinking it were morning I could hear men's voices quite clearly in earnest discussion. But my memory is poor and I do not remember him speaking much with me. Oh I were beaten often enough when I were lax in my chores he had harsh words for me then but I cannot think of so many times when

46

he sat and conversed with me I cannot think of good things he told me the voice as I remember it is angry. I were young though when he went and perhaps it is no wonder. Still I am not sure he had much capacity for youth he were likely preoccupied with his own struggles. It is a strange thing and I have come to realize it late because now all his boys are grown and become men and we cannot learn what he would have thought of us.

Once when I were sick as a child he came into the room I shared with my brothers where I lay chilled in bed too weak to make myself warm. There had been a lot of sickness that year there were friends of mine who died in the winter for want of strength and heat no doctor came to save them just the waiting arms of angels to carry them up. I remember when I were well again and met with my classmates and we were fewer in number. It were a harrowing time full of grieving and sadness it pains me that I no longer own the names of those who were taken.

I had it worse than my brothers I were smaller than them with less resistance and my mother were almost as sick with worry for me. But he had come in and laid his hand on my forehead and though I had a fever that hand seemed hotter still and he pressed in on my skull as though he would squeeze it from me this sickness and he prayed. He knew what it were to suffer and had great sympathy for those in illness he knew how often they go forgotten.

And of my grandfather nothing. Nothing other than he worked at the mine face. That he preached and it were a better time for the Church then. I have heard many stories of how yesterday the Lord worked wonders in our land of multitudes gathering eager for the Word but that yesterday were a long time ago and seems to have belonged to some other place. If my father were a keen historian of our chapels he were no keeper of family history and passed little down to me that I can record. My mother knows more than I do I will remember to ask her when I am able to return I hope it will not be long away. The past is too soon lost. I feel a need to keep it from eternity.

I prayed in this way a long time giving thanks for all my blessings I kept my eyes shut so that the darkness which met me when I opened them were unexpected the candle had burned itself out and were cold beside me. I felt for the first time the nervous fatigue in my limbs and realized how exhausted I were that the day had been a trial and though it had been pleasantly done I would not have much sleep before I had to get up again. I finished with the Lord's Prayer felt God to be with me then lay down in my bed bringing up my knees until I fitted in.

I closed my eyes and saw in the black flashes of white light like fireflies though my room dark and no light entering in. A curious trick of my tired eyes. A late breeze of spring air found its way into the room and blew across my face I felt something unspeakable to be contained within. Some fragrance which struck me something which spoke in a quiet voice promising the nearness of summer. Not from a particular plant I could name but a mixture of scents all things combining sweetly together. Well it were too early in the year still and such plants could not have been there for me to smell but I knew them intimately I did not think I were mistaken. So it were a strange thing. And perhaps it were my tired state or because I had been dwelling on my father while I prayed but it came like a crack in my heart bringing memories of summers past. When we were children playing on the green after chapel. How free we were. The days lit with gold. Games of king of the castle in the trees beside the farmhouse the great joy I took in sports the shared pleasure we had in them. I thought that the sweetness of the air must be exactly as it were then to cause this sudden rush of remembering.

How sad it is past. The days offered themselves as though they would never end we imagined the world a safer place than the one we have inherited a joyful world alive on top of this one it seemed true though it exists no longer.

The past is a small domain. Its boundaries are thin and close. Would that I could live there always and not be left to yearn for what I felt then. But I knew this were only a sleeping desire. I have my Lord for company *he* has travelled this way with me. And though I might miss my friends there are many among them who are gone into eternity and the places we played are now distant the games no longer fit for me. For man awakes and responsibilities are laid upon him he has no time for the idle pleasures of youth it would be foolishness when we have our Salvation at stake. All I have for solace are the memories of play they are dear to me but saddening.

And these were the thoughts that took me quickly from my waking. So it were a strange day full of blessing but I am not sure if I were glad or unhappy when I went to sleep and I do not remember my dreams so I do not know if they contained a sign which might have given me the answer.

9

Another winter has finally turned over and much is gone with it. I should be glad but there is something in its passing which unsettles me I am brought to remember that I will see so few summers and winters and that each new one is closer to the last. April has arrived and the new season burst with speed upon us. The green is come to its home the flowers sprung up with bright hosannas of purple and white.

Well I have not had much time to admire the spring the week has been spent at work amid the smells of coarse smoke and new metal. It chokes me when I come in and burns away slowly. Takes an hour or two before I am breathing deeply again this last year has seen my lungs grow used to the heat my skin hardened by it. And I am accustomed too to the rote. I did not think I would have much liking for it but I have been shown again that I were wrong about my character. There is a rhythm of work that carries me through the day the heavy ringing note constant as a heartbeat patterning my actions and consuming my thoughts so that the day passes rapidly. It feels good. My attention taken up with it. Nothing else keeps in my mind but it is a noble state to be in it seems to balance my soul and set things right it is very rewarding.

The tasks too have their fascination for me. There is the fire which must be set at the correct heat a more difficult skill than I imagined. I have only lately grown sensitive to the subtle colours of the flames. Then watching the metal heat until the colour is right and freeing the hammer in my hand to fall through the air and bring temper to the iron my other hand gripped on the tongs holding the metal fast to catch the hammer blow. Three hard beats and then turning it to catch the fourth. Two more beats then turning it again. The tongs are a simple tool two long pieces of metal jointed close to one end but delicate instruments now that I handle them right.

When I began my time here the arm that held the hammer alternated between limpness in the day when I almost felt too weak to keep swinging and then extreme stiffness on the night so much so I were barely able to move. There were long weeks I had sharp cramps shooting pains in my shoulder and chest I could hardly work the bellows. My shoulder muscles are tightened now and expanded in knots the hammer has grown lighter so I have come to treat it as nothing other than a more solid part of my own arm. My blistered hands are healed the skin toughened like canvas inured to easy burning. I give my body over to the work burn with a fierce sweat in recognition of the exercise and a hard-won weariness at the end of the day. It would be very harsh labour indeed if I always gave thought to how much I had to do the tasks would grow heavier I do not think my will would be strong enough to do it afresh every day but in the right mind I can work hour after hour and not be much tired until the end.

Yesterday it were farriery there were horses to shoe a long line of them waiting their turn. I were amused to see some of the farmhands who had brought them not prepared to wait until we were done so they left the horses tethered and when I had finished shoeing them I were expected to lead them back on the road and set them off along it from where they would find their own way home. And they do it quite happily each going in its right direction it is a strange sight to see these heavy burden horses trotting along alone and unbridled.

It is good to work with the earth. Its materials and the beasts on it. My life before this were in farming and that too were a brutal life but I miss the animals and it were good to spend time in the fields to be out beneath the sky. Still I am come to see that my future will be here now. It will be another year before my apprenticeship is finished and I might have some proper income. Over half my earnings now are spent on food I have had just bread and cheese wrapped up for lunch the same every day this week and I have found myself feeling quite hungry. My temporal worries are a great distraction for me sometimes I feel paralysed when I think of everything I would like to have to be comfortable and how far away it seems. It lays a great weight on my life it feels that it will drag me down through the soil to the Inferno that I will be left hungry and without a home. Indeed there are times here when my eyes are watering with smoke and the fires are burning hot the coals crooked and glowing with toothed caverns and the forge looks like nothing so much as a vision of the flames of Hell itself.

But it does not do me too much good to spend my hours here absorbed in thought. A week or so past I lost myself in pumping the bellows thinking about my income and how I might improve my position and in allowing these worries to come into my mind I had warmed up quite a blaze without noticing. Just watching the colours turn and letting the fire grow too hot burning white in the centre. And I stood there dumbly until I had caused a hot spark to spit from the furnace it caught me on my cheek just by my eye left a burn mark there and I were lucky it were not a half-inch higher. My apron is scalded with similar burns the leather marked by too many errors. It reminds me how much I am blessed. These small things transpire and we think little of them but I have remembered to give thanks because it is proof to me that God offers us protection even when we do not have *him* in our thoughts. We are so ignorant of these things.

The smith here is Mr Coad my instructor. He owns the old forge and the cottage beside it both he has a wife and two young daughters who have come late in his life. But he is clearly satisfied with his lot which is much better than many have. It is a profitable enough place there is plenty of business enough work for the two of us. And I cannot help but think that presently he has the benefits of my labour without much compensating me.

When he sets his tools aside at the end of the day and leaves me to blunt the fire and close the place he walks to the stream to wash and then turns to his house and does not look back at his work having put it cleanly from his mind. And I think that there is much to be imitated in his life besides his expertise at work. I find myself quite desirous of his security but it seems a long way off and the future has not much to offer except more of the work I have already had.

He is a very generous man I think but quiet and not much given to the use of lectures as part of his instruction. It is a very different apprenticeship from that I have had under Mr Roberts who liked to spend a great deal of time talking. When Mr Coad has something to show me he will call me over and demonstrate quite swiftly the task in hand without explanation and I am expected to know it. Well this system of his has its flaws it has resulted in some wrongdoing on my part there have been things I were not too sure of and so I have had reason to feel ashamed but I am quite taken with it. And the truth is that all the failings are my own they represent nothing other than my inability to correctly resemble the example set me. I have been pondering over a lesson in it an image that I will call on for a sermon that we are set the task of imitating our Master and that perhaps we would be better doing less preaching and more in the way of action showing our love of God with our deeds. And then I were entertained with the thought because I would find myself preaching *for* action and *against* preaching which did not seem such a good outcome it presented quite a problem for the sermon and I have puzzled over it. So that were not quite the lesson I had in mind but there were something in there. The role of the preacher is to illuminate Christ so that others might imitate *him* and not to shirk action ourselves. And I were rueful at the thought because I am not one to neglect my duties I do a fair share already and could scarcely do more.

So that were the week it were hardly leisured. Because I were tired I have slept a great deal as much as I were able and not had much time to myself. I went out early on Tuesday to change the tracts. There were a prayer meeting on Thursday but it were poorly attended and seemed almost a waste of my time. Still I have put aside an hour each evening to read from the Bible and Friday after work I found an hour to call upon Harriet French so I have had some profit from the week.

10

I had but a little time with Harr her cough came and were resilient it did not settle down easily. She apologized she said she were very tired and needed to sleep a little so I left her there and went to talk with her mother so that we might pray together.

William had appeared at the door while I were with her and he walked me downstairs. He were of an unusually talkative disposition he is normally quiet and shy during my visits. But he were telling me that he had taken up fishing in the woods and asking if I knew much about it and would I like to come sometime.

We came into the kitchen and still he talked it appeared he intended to carry on this way and not leave us much space nor quiet for prayer. So I told him I did not have long to visit and should spend that time with his mother so perhaps he should wait with Harriet and watch in case she awoke and required him. I felt a little bad after that because it deflated his spirit and I saw the disappointment in his face as he went from the room but I thought he would understand that my duties were important and I could not waste time talking of idle things.

Mrs French asked me how Harriet had been and I said well I thought. Then we sat quietly in the kitchen it were a comfortable rest the room is to my liking it does not feel like I am sitting in a stranger's home. She fetched some water for me to drink. I reminded myself of the surroundings. There is a painting of her done which sits usually on the wall upstairs but a few weeks ago they moved it here beside the kitchen window and I like to look on it while I visit. I have asked Harr about it she knows it and can picture it well in her mind so I have heard the story. It were a painter that visited once and portrayed her mother in the kitchen chair. There are no other people from this village that have paintings of them there are none that can afford them so it is quite a rare thing and a tremendous vanity. Yet I am told he left the painting without asking a fee. If it were worth something I am sure they would have sold it by now but it is of no one and who would want it?

In the picture she sits by the table and the window is open and lets in the light it is a bright day outside. I wonder why he did not paint her outside for the colour. It is so pale and watered. She sits not to look at the painter but across the table at something we cannot know. She is wrapped in her shawl and seems an old woman though you cannot clear see her face it is loosely done. Perhaps the painter did not have an eye for the detail of faces. Still you have to marvel at the art of it how he looks and puts what he sees on the canvas.

Sometimes when I visit and we sit here the widow sits the same way in the tiny kitchen and watches to see that the stove does not burn out even as I look at her image behind her. The wood burnt in the kitchens is what William fetches from the grounds of the big house as with many of the poor families here he is allowed to collect anything dead and on the ground there are many who survive on such pickings. The fire in the other room is never lit just warmed by the rising heat of smoke in the chimney. Coal is near one shilling a bag and they cannot afford it not even coal dust to warm the sick. Harr's room is cold in winter our breath often visible while we talk. They heap her bed with rags so she has some weight to lie beneath. The window shutters fasten with ties but the frame is poorly fixed perhaps warped with damp and lets in a draught. Sometimes her mother carries her to the kitchen for warmth wrapped in a blanket from the bed and we sit by the stove together William too if he is here though the kitchen is fair full with us all in.

And they survive off very little the giving of the circuit and a few labours. There are some potatoes tilled in the garden.

William collects wood and sheep's wool from the hedges I would not think he could gather enough to spin it. In season they gather flowers for money irises and Double Whites a useful source of income for many families in these parts but not enough for the year. The effects of this poverty are clear I have seen the worst of it in Harr but there is something appalling in that she who suffers most is given to have most faith in her Saviour I am brought to tears thinking on it.

When I think of my own circumstances I am much ashamed for I have received many blessings from the Lord and yet I do not always feel I have happiness in my heart. I were reminded of the lesson I had prepared for the children of the widow in the temple and sure in my heart is this knowledge that the beauty of their gifts does not lie in their wealth.

I sat with Mrs French we spent a short time in prayer and then before I left we returned a while to talking. I did not plan on sitting there with her for long. But it turned out she had been wanting to speak with me so I stayed to listen and it seemed that Harr's tiredness had perhaps been sent to provide us with the opportunity. She had worries she wanted to ask me about and they were over William she said he had been something of a burden to her of late. It is sad he misses his father's guidance he has not had much direction and I think things would be very different for the boy if he had.

He is too old to be schooled now she said. He says we need his income and will find work for himself. I have kept him from the mines because I have been afraid of losing him. But I know they will have him there.

Well I did not doubt it but it is not good work.

I have forbidden him but I cannot make him obey me in this she said.

And I were astonished to hear that. He is a young boy still and a respectful one I had thought.

He would disobey you? I asked. I am certain he wouldn't.

He has grown independent the last months. He wants his freedom and he will not do what I ask of him. I have been caring for Harriet and not had much time for him. I had hoped . . . Well. I had hoped others might find time for him.

I am sure you are wrong about him. And you should keep him from the mines. It is not right for him. He benefits greatly from his classes still and he could do better. We should trust in the Lord to provide. There will be something else that arises I am sure of it.

What though? she asked and I did not know.

Well I promised her that I would set some time aside to have words with him and ask him to consider his behaviour. I think it is selfish of the boy with his sister lying in sickness he should be helping his mother more and looking to assume his responsibilities. He could not go to the pits. The thought offered a painful vision to my mind. That it would be as it had been with her husband. Wives sit in their kitchens and await the tolling of the bell that warns there has been an accident at the mine. It is not such a rare sound. And what must it conjure for those who have loved ones there?

We prayed then for her circumstances and afterwards I asked her a little more about them I did not think things were well at all. It seems the estate has reduced her rent to accommodate her so that she has somewhere to live but it is a temporary situation brought about because of her daughter's sickness she will not be treated so fairly in the future. When Harr is gone into eternity I think she cannot stay here but the almshouses are already full of widows so I do not know what home she will find.

I had thought spring were here some weeks past but the weather has been cold again and fierce a sharp wind from the north. We had this for almost two weeks it has blown most of April away with it and has only now turned. It is our first sunny day for a long time. But the Word says that *In the midst of life we are in death* and we cannot escape the evidence of its truth. I record the names of some that are gone into eternity. For this is how it shall be saith the Lord *Whoever shall seek to save his life shall lose it.*

Mr Blackmore died God rest his soul he dropped in the road by his door walking out to meet his daughter.

Albert Kelly from Menheniot is dead by work crushed beneath a rock.

Three men are dead in the Prince of Wales mine two of them brothers lost beneath a collapsing roof and drowned in the slime God rest their souls.

Muriel Webber is gone into the Lord with sickness.

A Mrs Lawry died in childbirth and her child with her no good death waited on them.

Blessed are the dead who die in the Lord.

Yea saith the Spirit that they may rest from their labours and their works do follow them.

So Mr Blackmore has passed away he were aged fifty-three years. It is no great age but there are few who work in the mines that last so long it seems that he were afforded a portion of his reward on this earth. His lungs had long been weak burnt thin by the fumes of industry but he suffered his lot without complaint and his last years contained many riches. We had his funeral two days ago so he is in the ground now. I needed to work additional hours in the week to be free for it but it were worth the labour we had a pleasant service the weather continuing fine.

When we assembled outside I met with his daughter and we talked for a while. Naturally she were given to grieving but she seemed a kind lady she is long married and gone to live with her husband in Liskeard I did not ask his profession. I wonder what it felt like for her to return to this village now that she has her place in town.

I told her of her father's faith how I had enjoyed his company. That I had confidence he were truly saved and had exchanged worlds for a better place. It is a strange loss to me though because I were a regular visitor to him and knew him quite well. So part of my weekly routine will be missing and no doubt I shall feel disorientated for a while. I am sorry I did not visit him again before he went.

The minister provided a good sermon we stood around the grave and sang our hymns. Mr Pendray read the lesson from Matthew 28th Chapter he had known Mr Blackmore from Church. His reading voice seemed thin as paper a cracked note of wavering pitch. I am reminded he is a few years older than Mr Blackmore were and appearing more fragile as the weeks go by.

Are you well? I asked after we were done.

A little tired he admitted. It is a sad occasion to come out for. I hope I do not have to attend too many more similar. I have seen enough of my friends buried.

We stood talking as the small congregation thinned and the graveyard emptied. Then I walked my Godfather to the station for his train home waited with him in the last of the sun and helped him board when it came.

Thank you he said it seemed a duty well performed.

God keep you I said. And the day had not been a sad one at all.

The week following has passed swiftly away and I am glad that I have had time to myself at the end of it. It is rare I have a day free from work that is mine to own when the hours were not filled with duties. But I knew the day were due so last week I have sent a message with the postman to James and asked if he would spend the day with me and were pleased to receive an answer. We have named this coming Saturday as free time together and arranged to meet I greatly look forward to it.

13

I rose early this morning a little after five. There were some cold water set aside to wash in. A little of the fish and potatoes from last night left over I ate some then wrapped the rest to take with me. And while the village were still quiet I set out to walk on the hill for long weeks I have been too busy to do so. The year is growing fine and I gained warmth in the walking and were able to reflect on the changing seasons. Spring has set now and we are on the edge of a full summer the green increasing in volume and filling out the land. The hills seem like a proper home for our Lord and I love to visit them early when they are empty of people. The air new and fresh and I the first to breathe of it.

When I left the cottage there were a damp white mist over the village my footsteps fell with an odd echo between the hedges. It were a disconcerting sound it made the world around me have the feel of a dream as though I might awake and find the skies clear and myself far away from here. But as the light grew and the sun burned through the cover the mist rolled away as if brushed back by a divine hand. It brought a radiance to the whole valley. A verse came to my mind and though I cannot recall its provenance it lodged there I thought on it many times in the day *Truly the light is sweet and a pleasant thing it is to behold the sun.*

I started from home heading north-east my aim were to meet James by Newbridge and walk with him in the hills over to the Tamar then follow the river south and come in by St Germans Quay. I left Quethiock from the small green where the village cross stands an ancient Celtic marker its wheelhead cross patterned like woven flax the dark granite stained with patches of yellow lichen. I went along the graveyard wall of the parish church it sat still and quiet in the mist a little ghostly. There is a Wesleyan chapel at the end of the lane but it is unused since my grandfather's time the congregation no longer enough to support it. Likely there are still debts on the buildings. Some from the circuit come to take care of it so it is kept in good condition and it waits there expecting revival prepared for the return of the Spirit in this place.

And then the village were behind me I opened up my stride to keep warm and went quickly down the lane. The roadside here is high hedges and thick with brambles in a few months they will ripen fully I had a sudden longing for their sweet taste. They are man-made these hedgerows built from earth and turf heaped over a stone heart but are grown wild with grass and flowers there is purple tufted vetch at the grassy foot laddered pea flowers and campion strewn around quite a chaos of colour. They would grow quickly over the whole road I think they would do well in the mud but it is kept in check by our trampling it down and the passing carts cutting a way through for us when they come. Swallows arched above the fields their curving flight swift and strong.

It were good to be removed from dry routine and come face to face to meet with God. There are times I feel how close I am to being bound by dull habit. As much hope as I have in the Church there are those who live at second hand and though they hear the Word of the Lord they do not look for the voice that speaks it. It is refreshing to have a communication with *him* unmediated by dry barriers. Here in these grounds in the quiet moments on mine own the sun on my skin I can pray and absorb *his* Creation. It is so quiet of people the noises are sweeter and more intelligent it seems.

James were waiting for me by the mill pond at Newbridge the same as he had in years gone by. We fell into an even step together. I had been expecting we would launch into talk believing we had plenty to catch up on but we set off in silence and I could not think how to start our conversation.

63

Our relationship has changed a little it seems and it will take a short while before we are entirely comfortable in our company again. I thought it were partly that I no longer knew who we were and I must first ask myself that before we could talk. In any case we strode along in companionable silence and I feel that perhaps the familiarity will return.

We left the lanes near Newbridge went through the small wood there coming out onto the moor where the land begins to rise. There were rabbits running in all directions. We heard curlews out low over the heath making their strange call. Felt the heather sprung beneath our feet an old sensation from my childhood the soft grasses just as I remember them. And there is gorse speckled around early in its yellow a pleasant sight bright and familiar.

I nearly stepped into a marshy pond but saw it just in time there were damson flies mating over it locked together in clumsy flight. Yellow irises at the edge. We followed the valley up where the stream cuts sharply into the slope the water looks clean enough but with runoff from the mines I would not trust it. They extract copper and tin above here lately wolfram too and there is arsenic in huge amounts in the form of mispickel which they formerly piled on waste heaps but which Mr Blackmore once informed me they now export to America. He had a long life working in the ash heaps and though he is gone from us until the end he liked to talk about the mines and he knew what went on there daily even to tell me which men were working in which pit. He gained great pleasure from sharing his gossip I think it made him feel as though he were still among them.

Ascending the hill the breeze were fiercer than I had anticipated the low ground we had come through had been well sheltered. The air a strengthening valley wind blowing upwards and at the lip where the line of the rise disappeared from sight it cooled into clouds. I were pleased to see it for I had left my cap behind and it meant a cool climb without the sun on my head. And near the top of the hill when we were beneath the thickest cloud a short shower came over us it were a refreshing sensation these drops on our faces do a lot to remind us we are alive and part of the world composed ourselves from clay and heavenly breath. I know many people who will not go out in the rain they associate it with unhappiness but it is a mystery to me it causes me a very great happiness indeed swelling up from my stomach a bubbling sensation in my chest. With no good reason I laughed out loud I am usually alone and do not want to look too foolish but with James I were in excellent spirits and felt no need to restrain it. I think James were not so fond of rain as I am but he could not help but join my laughter. We were left a little wet but not drenched and not cold neither and our shirts would dry soon enough.

Then on the hilltops the cloud fell apart a ragged edge torn off by the stronger wind it gusted around and caught in my ear so strangely that I thought someone had leaned close by to whisper to me.

We walked a long while following the line of the peaks though in truth there is nothing more here than a few gentle hills. But the valleys slope down a long enough way and the effect on the views is considerable it provides the impression of greater depth than there is.

Climbing Kit Hill we came across the open ground staying away from the mine chimney on its peak. It is an impressive landmark a tall finger on the land built of blackened brick the tower bounded with iron belts. The engine house stark on the moor. Lodged there solidly as though it had sent deep roots down into the soil. Well it is an unnatural growth on the land no doubt the earth feels the shock of its presence. I wonder will it ever be removed and the land reclaimed for itself.

We turned our backs on the mine and looked out. The views from here are the most beautiful I know they make me wish I could come more often. The high moors far to the west appeared black and shadowed even in the sun. Around beneath the hill perhaps twenty farms in clean sight only a keen eye were required to pick out their walled bounds and the flocks out to graze. Far east on the horizon were Dartmoor but nearer to us the wide reach of the Tamar opened out in the green meandering between rounded spurs. I thought now it would be too far to walk that way today because we had wandered a long time in the hills and not come as straight as we had set out to do.

We stood there taking in the wealth of it.

Look there James said. Do you see them?

I followed his arm. Saw a pair of buzzards in the sky. We watched them wheeling in the air the fingers of their wings outstretched reaching to trace the breeze. And I were made sad to think that no one else had come to see the views.

I feel ashamed now for the great poverty of my imagination to keep in my mind that beauty as it were presented us. And shame for the poverty of my speech to take hold of it and describe it. The sensations are beyond me I am a simple man unfit for beauty and grace. It is the same when I preach when I am struggling to prepare my sermons I have no great grasp of words that I can tell of all I know of *his* love for us.

I feel there is much to be learned from the sights not merely the beauty of the surface of our canvas here a beauty no painter could have the skill to reproduce. But because I am gone there right in the mind of God I am enabled to see the depth of all things. How God and the world are one that this natural land is a proper representation of *his* order prevailing and all this a part of it even I. Heaven resides under our feet as well as over our heads. The feelings that are caused to rise in me here meet exactly the impressions I have of my Lord so that my sense of *him* within is given full balance by the evidence of *his* work without. It is a powerful revelation of *his* presence. That this world is mere shadow except that our Lord inhabits it. That the trees are brought to breathe by *his* Divinity in them that the very life of us all is that part of *his* Nature which *he* has provided us.

66

Men who are impoverished in the spirit and much afflicted by doubt go to search for God in dry books or close themselves off in thick-walled churches as if *he* hides there well their blessings are few if they cannot see evidence of *him* in all things. Oh Lord let us not become a part of the shadow but have full life with *you* and *your* peace in our hearts.

There are many who seem to behave as though the world were their own work wrought of their own hands. And yet I have seen how those that have not love for their Lord come to despise themselves and their works and treat all that surrounds them with contempt. So there in that blessed state I thought with strong anger of all those proud men who come with their books and theories and tell us that *his* Word is lies and that we worship in vain for there is no God. All those clever men whose brains decry their hearts whose learning has left them foolish so they no longer know that the test of faith is not found at school or by evidence but on the pulse's steady beat where we feel the truth in the heat of our blood.

We were both sated by the visual feast we had been provided and we remarked on how glorious it seemed. Conversation seemed to come more easily after that. As we talked we looked to go south towards Landrake it is not a path I have taken often but the way is easy to find. There are stannaries at intervals whose chimney stacks serve as waystones it would be impossible to lose yourself you could make a jagged journey across the countryside connecting such markers though it were not the quickest path.

We left the hill and walked south down over the rolling green until I grew tired. It were good to stretch my legs I stand so much at work I do not want to grow stiff and let my muscles forget what it is to reach. But after we had followed the path nearly as far as Landrake the tall church tower visible and close above the trees they began to pain me a sharpish ache behind my knees and we stopped there.

I'm aching James I said. I'm too tired from work I think. I should find my way home.

Well he said I'm glad to hear it. I thought you were going to walk me into the ground. I'm tired myself but didn't want to say.

I thought that were not entirely true he seemed not in the least bit weary. He looked at the sky.

We have been out a long time he said. Will you make it home all right?

I'll be fine. It's not too far. We have enough light yet.

We gathered our breath.

It's good to do this again isn't it? I said to him.

Good yes he said.

I do not think there will be too many more times.

Perhaps. It is not like when we were young. And perhaps we shall marry soon.

Oh is there someone then? I asked affecting to hide my interest.

He laughed and said well yes he were optimistic. And I were quite happy for him though a little envious too because he seemed to be living a different life from the one I did wherein different things were possible.

We parted there and promised ourselves to do it again soon. He returned northwards along the Lynher and I went on into Landrake to cross the river and join the road to St Germans. I could feel the discomfort in my legs and were mindful that I had duties to go to the next day and so should have turned home. But I were sad to end the day too soon. I felt like a child who is called by his mother but does not respond for love of the delights he has found playing in the woods.

At a crossroads I stopped uncertain for a moment of my direction and saw a wayside tract it looked so old I were not even sure I recognized the lesson it contained. It must have been posted there for many months perhaps longer and I wondered whose duty it were to come here and why they neglected it. I regretted not having a spare tract on me. It is true I could volunteer myself at the next distributors' meeting but it feels like I have all I can do at the moment and the post is some way out of my area. If it fell only on me to do my duties I would surely fail I am grateful for the strength of God to support me in it. Well I would bring it up at the meeting and perhaps it would rouse someone to own it. But it were a sad thing to find on the way.

My legs ached harder on the road causing me to shorten my stride. I have need of more exercise but I know I should measure it out and take care not to harm myself. Still I knew my Lord were watching over me because the tide had come in pushing the river higher and when I came to St Germans Quay from the wrong side I were able to call for a boat to ferry me across the Tiddy it saved me a walk up the bank again to the railway bridge.

By St Germans I were in need of a rest and were glad to have the opportunity to visit some of the sick and needy in the parish it meant that the day were not spent entirely on myself.

There were one especially I were glad to see. Her mother and brother were both absent I let myself in the house I have done it before though this were the first occasion when I had not made a prior arrangement to come. Harr did not seem to mind she were lying quietly in bed and seemed tired but pleased to welcome me. She did not have the breath for talking so I sat with her a while in a pleasant silence. And though she were not well her spirit seemed quite content. Still I did not stay too long her sickness is severe and she cannot endure much company.

Met Dr Coryton our local practitioner on my way out. He had been fetched by Mrs French who were following him home some way behind. His is not a local name he is from some way to the east beyond Plymouth I think and so a Saxon the differences are plain to see in his face. He had a cheerless manner too he said that there were little to be happy for here that the girl were very sick and would soon die.

And I thought how blind can he be how much faith can he have in bodies and what he knows of them when he cannot even see how happy she is how strong her soul and ready for the Lord there is nothing to be sad for here just the ignorance of man. If her frame is weak it does not matter because it has been a perfect mould for the Lord to cast in *he* has poured the strong iron of faith through it and all that is lasting here will endure.

14

That evening were warm and heavy the scent of rain and new grass blowing sweet from the meadows. I took deep breaths of the fragrance it were a heady feeling and seemed to heighten my joy. The sky still blue and darkening but not yet night. The moon already evident close to full and low in the south. A bright star emerging beneath it and left.

I have a strong liking for the longer days as we come into summer and how quiet the land seems it settles down like an animal to sleep in the late warmth. Sometimes I can almost sense the earth lift the gentle breathing of it a rocking in the ground beneath my feet.

So it were a beautiful day everything seemed to be singing the praises of its Creator but then I am returned to town and take my eye from Nature to look on our own imperfections it is a disappointing sight. Close to home I came by two drunkards they were in bad repair and very loud as they went arm in arm so I were briefly concerned. I have had such encounters before and find them uncomfortable. I did not want to attract their attention or suffer their violence. Well it turned out I did not have any need to worry because they were too drunken to threaten much violence to anyone.

I averted my eyes as I went past them wishing to show them my disapproval. So I were not looking as we drew level and the slighter of the two tottered away from his friend and reeled suddenly into me. I felt a rush of fear when he hit me sudden excitement in my chest thinking I were being attacked but it were quite unintentional on his part I think he were the victim of the drink he had taken and the malice were not his own merely that of the spirit that held him. He sprawled on the floor by my feet I smelt the ale stink of him as he fell. And then I bent down and lifted him up saw drying stains on his coat. The worsening acid sweet smell of vomit. I felt deep shame at his situation but anger too and I were not afraid to have words with him. I wanted to offer him some correction but he were in no state to listen and his friend had stopped and were watching to see what I did. There were a fearful look in his eye as though he had been woken up and found himself suddenly backed against a wall I saw desperation swimming slowly in his mind past the drink. Well I realized then that I were a clear head taller than either of the two and perhaps they were more afraid of me than I had thought. So I held his friend off the ground and shook him a little but felt quickly ashamed by the harshness of the gesture and left him standing. Then I turned and walked on not looking to see if his partner had caught him before he fell again.

Drink is a terrible curse. They destroy themselves and some seem happy to do so well perhaps they should have damnation if it is what they want but they have no right to take their families with them. We have enough poverty already the land is stricken with it and it is a mortal sin to aid its progress to invite it to your family's table and share it out with them as though it were food to live from. I have seen the trouble drink has caused and have a hatred of the stuff. I have often been to the temperance meetings to hear speakers they have a worthy cause and have saved some few.

Not only the meetings would be good for those sinners. I were made to feel sad again that the hills today had been empty of these people I think it would do much good for them it would teach them to lift their eyes from the ground from the temptations they have close to hand and look instead into the long distances.

I saw my landlady at the end of the day. She were in the kitchen sitting straight on the wooden chair its tall rounded back reaching high over her head. She seemed lost in thought beside the smoky range the atmosphere were close and unpleasant after so much fresh air today. A sheet of paper lay folded beneath her hands. She asked what I had been doing all day and when I answered the reaction in her face were so clear that she did not need to tell me that she thought I had wasted the hours her silence tasted bitter it were full of disdain. Sometimes her contempt for things runs deep it comes easily from her. But I thought then what had she been doing that were worth more? Perhaps she had not even been outside. For she eyes the things she has and looks only so far as to see the objects she covets. It must be a small and lonely world to inhabit.

We sat in the kitchen for a while in the evening but we were silent neither of us much disposed to talk and I came to feeling quite uncomfortable so in a short time I left her and went to read my Bible with my mind on the class tomorrow. I had my teaching duties to fulfil another Sabbath that had come quickly round. The hours I had for sleep were short and I rose early.

15

Several unhappy weeks have passed since that glorious day lost to the monotony of work and I have only now found my way to visit Harriet French again. I found their house quite busy with activity the hillside crop of Double Whites had flowered and they had been picking them in the week. Mrs French apologized and brought me into the kitchen where she and William were busy with the work of sorting and bunching. Half-curled in a chair in the corner were Harr she greeted me her voice sounded tired. William did not look up he remained absorbed in his work. It had been a good yield it seemed for it is often an unreliable plant which grows blind and flowerless and some years is in short supply in the markets. But today blooms draped off every surface. Their fragrance so thick we seemed to breathe of the flowers themselves. Well it were a beautiful sight but funereal too. They will be sold to the market I hear that soon with the railway they will be able to transport them to London for the markets there and people speak hopefully of it for it promises better income. I imagine they are starved for flowers in the city. Here we are merely starved for want of work or money and all this beauty will not feed us.

I'm sorry Mr Wenmoth Mrs French said. We're quite busy with this. I could make some tea for you.

No no I said. I thought I might help.

And they made room for me at the table.

But my hands it transpired were ill suited to the task I thought I were quite dextrous but it seemed I did not have the required skill it were new to me and they are delicate things and would not bundle together as I willed them without stems breaking. It did not seem like such a difficult thing but

I suppose there is more skill involved than I gave credit for. I found it to be a frustrating occupation and I did not have much patience for it.

I watched Harr. She did not seem well. Her eyes were bruised with tiredness the skin beneath them darkening in half moons like metal beaten and stained with soot.

I think Mrs French realized my efforts were doing more harm than good and kindly invited me to rest from them and keep Harr company while she and William worked. So I ceased with bunching and left it to mother and son they worked swiftly with practised hands and left me feeling a little ashamed. I took my stool over to sit by Harr and in our quiet corner of the kitchen by the stove we had some space to talk a little while the work progressed.

I asked her what the doctor had said when he last came though I did not trust him to have said anything of use.

She answered quite quietly. The same as he always says she said. You know what he says.

It were a calm answer and she avoided speaking the words only for politeness' sake there were no fear in it. The thought turned in my mind and I nearly did not speak it but I felt at ease with her and curious.

Are you afraid? I asked. Are you not afraid of dying?

I confess there were surprise on her face at the question and I thought perhaps it were not tactful of me.

Why should I be? she said. I cannot think of a reason.

She knew she went to a better place and it were a reprimand to me because she knows it in her heart and I must sometimes doubt just how clear that same knowledge sits in me.

She made to speak again but the words came pressured and whispering from her lungs then overtaken by harsh coughing. The scent of the Whites dense in the air I wondered if it did not contribute.

Her mother turned to us and said she thought it were better then if Harr lay down. I offered I should leave them that I were causing them trouble on a busy day but she said no and she did not object to me staying that I were welcome to talk or pray with the girl. So she and William carried her upstairs the cough accompanying her and laid her on the bed and I took the chair William offered me to sit on while they returned downstairs to continue the work. Through the open door I heard their voices continue in soft conversation below us.

At length the coughing fit passed. Harr lay limply on the bed quite exhausted it seemed. Those dark hollows by her eyes burrowing deeper into the pale but her lips curiously bright with colour.

Do you feel better? I asked.

Yes she said and a tired sigh came with the word. Thank you.

And then a moment later a note of her old self returned to her voice it were very cheering to hear and she asked Well what shall we talk about today?

Now I have long wondered how she came to know her Lord and love *him* with such passion. But she has seemed herself on the verge of Heaven and I were worried I would not get an account from her. So I am glad I found the courage to ask her then directly because she told me her story with a frankness I did not expect. Perhaps her suffering has provided her this maturity I think there are not many her age that could provide so straight an account of a difficult thing. I were pleased too because though I am not family she found it easy to confide in me and I do not think that were solely because I am with the Church.

For years she said she were convinced she were nothing but a sinner she attended Sunday School but nothing particular seemed to affect her. But she were sorry for her sins and when she were taken worse April three years past she became intensely concerned about her soul and sought pardon for her sins. So she struggled but could not find in herself belief in Jesus neither that *he* had died for her and she went on this way until late summer. And then one time came she said and she were wrestling in prayer all night and were visited by some evil spirit who stayed by her side for many hours. She experienced an appalling feeling of horror she said the sense that everything might be lost.

Well she says she did not know what it were she were feeling if not a spirit tormenting her so she thought she must have the courage to face it and she called this demon to come out. And because she called out with the name of our Lord which has dominion over all things the spirit obeyed.

It took on human appearance she said. The like of a large face in the darkness surrounded by cloud or smoke. A sulphurous smell emanating. The apparition wide-faced and waxen but ugly because it did not seem at all humanlike. It had an immense mouth that blew from it a fiery blast which threatened to carry her soul away and leave her in sin and chaos and that mouth opened further and massive until it folded out around and consumed even the face itself and its force grew stronger.

It were a powerful creature and seemed as though it would never leave but she continued in prayer and her Saviour came to the foot of the bed the rock of her Salvation and light shone around the room and she rejoiced. Afterwards there were bad air to be cleaned from the room and she says her whole bed had to be changed it were soaked through with the sweat of her battle. And I understood a little why nothing since has held much fear for her neither her suffering nor the closeness of Heaven for she won a great victory that day.

I were quite overwhelmed by her testimony it seemed a rare account of a battle fought for our Master and momentous too for the saving of *one soul* is without measure. And when she had finished I thought to tell her of my own conversion to the Lord. It is a glorious date and the promises I made on that day are fresh in my mind though it has been four years. But she were tired and I saw she needed rest that her story had taken much of her energy to tell. So I did not get an opportunity to share my story with her but the visit were nevertheless profitable. Her account has stayed with me powerfully since.

I think I might preach on it though I will not bring her name into it. I think we should all be motivated in the fight against such spirits. I feel I am closer to understanding her faith and our conversation has made me ache to talk with her more to return here soon and often and experience again the peace I feel in her company.

16

And yet it is not all peace I feel with her. In my gut there is an uneasiness about our time together there have been days the last months when I have been reminded that not all our communication is so true. Well those months have gone quickly from us. Summer has almost burned away June and July sweated from me in the seething heat of work. The air in the forge shimmers with the intensity of it and is thick with heat you cannot breathe of it you gasp for ice and there is only fire. My eyes have been afflicted by the smoke they have bled water until they were dry and could bleed no more.

Would that I could say then that during those days when I were free to visit with Harr there were occasions when we strolled in the garden to talk. Would that I could say that we left the garden and went along the lane and enjoyed some of the country together. I often imagine that we might someday do just that it would be a pleasant thing. But no it has remained the same as every other day previous I sit beside her bed and we suffice ourselves with speaking of those things which seem beyond our reach. We talk about what awaits us when our time comes.

It will be glorious to live in the kingdom she says.

Glorious yes. Though I would be sad to lose this world it is a beautiful place.

I think it cannot be so beautiful as what we are promised. Sometimes I feel as though I can see it.

And what do you see? I ask.

A bright light. Even now I see light sometimes. Odd flashes which appear directly in front of my mind. But this is quite different the light is constant and so bright I cannot look straight at it. And I know that *he* is there waiting for me. It is a very pleasant thing to think of it is a place I would happily go to.

And I remember how Moses veiled his face when he came down from Sinai for it shone with the light of the Lord and his people could not look on it.

I struggle though with her ease at the thought of death. She would forsake this world too gladly I think perhaps it is no surprise for she has already lost her sight of it. But she has pleasure in *him* now and in her family here too. And so much faith that better things await us nor any trace of bitterness at her circumstances. I thought on all the time she had lain here on this bed.

Do you not feel the time stolen from you? I ask.

A sound close to a laugh I do not know what it communicates.

I am happy for the quiet days she says. When things are not so distressed. When they are peaceful and I can rest and think a little. Or when William comes to sit with me. I like his company. He can make me laugh.

But the time is hardly your own I say. You cannot feel free.

It is a privilege to suffer for *his* name. I will be free soon enough.

So this is how it is. That she is content to wait patiently for the end. To desire the days dead to let them come short and quick and not give great care for their passing. Unmoved by the briefness of time possessed of the knowledge that she will be happy with her Lord.

And I feel strange pulls on me. For I too have a longing for that blessed state I have worked hard on this earth and am desirous of the rest we are promised. But I cannot help the fear I have for the end of things. Fear of losing what I have much of it is precious to me. How strange it is to experience these two sentiments so thoroughly though they seem to be in opposition to each other to long for Heaven but to yet feel horror as the days are lost.

That dread though is lessened in the time I spend with her. Our conversations of late have brought us much closer and I feel warmer for it and less inclined to fear. When she talks I can see her as she is her whole life I know her. It causes something to rise in me like a tide a flood of thanks it is so good to have such communion with another human soul God has blessed us to be so close. I do not need her to talk I could visit and sit in silence for a day and not need a word because of the fellowship we have in Christ. We gather in twos and threes and *he* is there *his* presence refreshing as rain in a hot summer.

There are times when she too rests in the silence and seems to feel the same as I. Only suffering can carry her so close to God. Would that I had the same faith I could move mountains. Never has the word of God been truer *If ye were blind ye should have no sin.*

But then I am reminded that she does not see me. When she tilts her head towards me it is to bend her ear to me and not her eyes. She cannot see me she cannot look in my eyes she cannot know me as I know her. Sometimes a worry creeps into my mind and plays there on my imagination and that is the thought that she talks to me as though I were her own creation which she has conjured into being and the delight she has in our company seems somehow to have nothing to do with me. I hear it in her talk she asks of me the wrong things she asks of the life of the Church and my life if she knew me she would not need to ask these questions. Perhaps she constructs my life from my voice not who I am and she imagines someone who is not like unto me perhaps someone who is older or someone who is strong in faith or someone who is kinder. I cannot explain it correctly this is not all I feel. It is simply that there have been occasions when I have been brought to doubting times when I have felt so rested and peaceful with her and have come to think that in those moments we have settled on something there together.

Then after I have been there a long while she starts as if wakening from a long sleep then breaks the silence and asks me a sudden question.

Are the roses in bloom now? she asks. Or

I think William shall soon be home she says.

And I discover that her mind were elsewhere and not in the places I thought it went. A great loneliness then settles on me as though I were suddenly removed from this world and her voice came from far away and spoke in a foreign tongue and that though I tried not to understand the words in my heart I did and they caused me to feel very sad.

17

There were finally though a day late in August when she were well enough to sit on a chair and be carried out into the garden though she were nervous. I do not know how long it had been since she last went outside perhaps years perhaps not since this illness first came upon her.

It will be a sweet day in my memory though it may be the last good day we have the last late heat of the year. It took a little persuasion before she agreed to come outside. We sat with her in her bedroom her mother and I only William absent. Her face were paler than ever. That room has made her fragile.

But do you really think I should? she asked.

Only if you wish to her mother said. But I think the sun might do you good if you do not get too much of it.

Perhaps we should have asked the doctor first Harr said.

And I thought then that she were not really worried for her health merely afraid at the prospect of treading outside again that there were something even in the idea of it that exhausted her.

She asked me what I thought and I said I felt it were a good idea and that she would only have to sit. I were keen she should breathe better air than she had in her room and it were a beautiful day outside.

I will find you a hat her mother said.

And when she had found the hat which were old just a piece of matted straw drooping with age and use we carried her out. Her chair so light I could have carried it myself without effort there were no weight to her at all.

In the garden the air were sweet we were overwhelmed by many scents that kept us from speaking for long minutes. I could sense the fine roses in the beds. The sweet smell of the plant my mother calls Traveller's Joy climbing through the garden twisting itself round the greenery. Felt the air contoured by the sounds of many insects. I saw Harr flinch at the warm touch of sunlight on her skin. I thought then that she knew her room too well and felt lost for a moment now she had come outside with her senses struggling to grasp the markers that would place her. Her head turned seeming to engage in twin designs trying to map out the garden without and manage the returning feelings within.

But she were quickened beside me. I heard her rapid breathing and the catch in it where her lungs tightened at the shock. Even sitting on the chair she reeled sideways her balance gone and she almost fell. But I were beside her and steadied her with a hand and leaned her back against the chair until she sat straight again on her own.

What is that smell? she asked. I know it but I have forgotten. It is not like the flowers for my room.

Perhaps the wild briars I said. Does it smell like the earth? Or Traveller's Joy. There is a lot of it here.

She repeated the name but did not say if I were right.

In the brightness I stared around and began to wonder if she might be perceiving the same colours her mother and I saw. It did not seem such a foolish idea I knew her vision were gone but thought that her mind might still summon them from memory. And I wondered what it were for her to be in this garden with the sight of it still in her recollection but only able to encounter it by its smells and sounds and with fingers that did not know their way. It seemed a strange and sad world a small place but even then I knew it felt too broad to her and full of fear and that she half longed to return inside.

Her mother picked a rose for her breaking off the thorns from the stem before placing it in her hand. She held it on her lap rubbing the petals gently between her fingers. Feeling the soft silk of it. It were a glorious day. The sun a pure coloured

84

liquid the cast and heat of metal ready to be worked. Even the edges of Harr's plain skirt in the sun flung in gold. For all her fear and discomfort in the open she looked untrammelled.

But she could not stay there too long and after a short while complained of a headache then began to cough it is a horrible sound. She held her handkerchief so tight across her mouth I wondered it did not aid the choking.

Mrs French came to help me with the chair but I felt I could carry it alone so I picked it up with Harr in it as though she were sitting in my arms. It were not so heavy the only trouble I had were in bringing her through the door I ducked low and cradled her as I bent. I took her up the narrow stairs felt the wooden steps give to take our weight her hands held the front of my jacket so she might feel secure though I would not have dropped her. The dying spasms of her coughing fit still wracked her jerking contractions of her body which she were too weak to resist.

So we returned in this way to her room and lifted her onto the bed where she breathed heavily it had taken such great effort. Her cheeks were flushed with the exertion I thought it a good sign but her mother were more concerned. She sat beside Harr and stroked her forehead. Her hair lay dead on the blanket the grey-brown of a rabbit's coat but long and fine.

She is so hot her mother said.

There were a red glow on Harr's face it seemed that there were something still vibrantly alive in her and perhaps she were not yet ready for the call. Her breath panting the air squeezing into her lungs a horrible groan. I held her hand awhile it were cold to the touch so refreshing I wanted to put it to my cheek but I were nervous to do so holding her hand this way were the first time and I have not touched her since. There were something so pure in the contact I can still summon the sensation of it. Her breathing slowed and became easier and I found myself breathing in time. Even as she suffers her grace seems to increase spreading around her and blessing those who come close.

85

She complained of pain in her chest and legs but did so sleepily the sentences muttered and dying on her lips. Her eyes flickered and looked through me then her lashes closed touching softly once and then again then finally a third time binding themselves shut.

I sat with her mother a while and we talked quietly it seemed we were all worn by the expedition though it had in truth been minor. Before I left she had words with me thanking me for the diligence of my duty for the time I had been giving them. But she expressed her worry that I were wasting my time that I gave her family too much of my day when there were so little hope.

What were my expectations? she kept asking.

And I have thought on that question many times since and still it saddens me. For Harr's life is in the Lord's hands and I am not a doctor that I can say yes yes I think she will recover or no there is no hope and all my prayers are not done for her recovery for she is far gone and close to God and I am just a man.

I met William on my way out as he came home. I were preoccupied from my conversation with his mother and I suppose my greeting of him were a little distracted. Then it were only after I were halfway from the village that I remembered I had promised his mother I would speak to him. That pledge were already long weeks overdue and it had slipped from my mind. I were annoyed with myself for forgetting I have been too crowded by duties of late.

18

I have had a hard week since then I have felt a slow anger in me and have struggled with it. There has been much to frustrate me it seemed as though every turn found me some new irritation I have tried to keep the annoyance contained in me but I wonder how long I can hold it before my thoughts are turned to bitterness. There are some things harder to forgive than malice and *thoughtlessness* is one of those. Why will they not set aside their childishness?

On Monday it were a man at the forge waiting for a horse and the animal were unhappy with its treatment it did not like being shoed. He had brought the irritable beast but clearly did not feel much like helping he stood aside with disinterest feigning not to see the troubles I had calming the animal when all that were needed were an extra hand on its mane and a word in its ear while I worked. I think I were lucky to escape being kicked and they give hard blows these beasts.

In the week I have been ashamed to see how many men neglect their dress. Well it cannot all be poverty because I am sure I do not earn more than they do but I am able to keep a clean set. They will not smarten themselves for the Lord they act like children never having learned to deny anything to themselves.

And then our reward the Sabbath wasted allowed to be lost and all its privileges with it. Just the emptiness of the churches and the sight of the congregations idle in their homes as I passed. Men playing marbles in the street for coins. My father had harsh words for those he thought were neglecting their duties I saw him take a stick to a man sleeping in the sun beside the church one day he berated him loudly as he beat him it were a most physical sermon. I do not have that same confidence to bring violence on the sinners and I am sure there will be some who think that means I am a lesser man than my father but that is not all it is for I know how hard their working days are and I too grow tired and sometimes it seems like I do not love the Sabbath as I should. So I will forgive them their rest but still I must condemn them for their sloth.

It were this I think that drew me into an argument with some men outside the church. We had gathered for our distributors' meeting for the tracts but the time were not profitably spent there were arguments over one patch two men not able to agree between them who would look after the area. Neither of them had other duties that would hold them from it they were merely trying to keep their own walks short and unwilling to go as far as their responsibilities required. And yet each were terribly high-minded in his talk well they are converted in their speech but not their hearts they do not own the Lord nor love these people enough.

So afterwards I decided to have words with them to say that they had wasted our time with debating trifles and prevented us from talking of more positive matters. Well if the subject had not been so serious I would have laughed at them for they did not take the criticism at all well. I think their anger hid a great deal of shame they lit up again in argument and complained at me. I offered them no response to it. Waited there for them to see their own foolishness. But they did not see. How is it they do not know the evil that afflicts them? They have lost their belief in it though it eats at them like a worm through earth and they are too easily given up to it.

I have beaten out my angers on the anvil I have doused them in the water bucket with the scalding metal as I cooled it hoping they would boil away with the steam. The scorching heat removed from me. And I have made my peace with the Lord each evening but then it is aroused again the next day and there is no end to the provocation I have been feeling.

There were a sad day in the middle of it too. I am gone down the quay to change the tracts and learned that a man were killed there in the morning. I missed his death but the pall of tragedy that visited the place were evident. It is the same each time it happens it has become too familiar a sight the strange peacefulness to the work as it continues an unnatural stillness to the mood. Normally it is a busy scene and loud too the works of the mines come to focus here and the boats that call are laden with ore and granite and lime there are shouts and cursing and the sounds of labour all around.

He had been caught in a tow line and dragged under the water. The man who worked beside him reached for him but he were too swiftly gone into the river the barges closing over him. They had retrieved his body had it lying under a tarpaulin waiting until the evening when the doctor could bring his cart and take it away. There were no one present to minister to him so I offered to pray over the body. I saw the remains his spirit gone from him his heavy face breathless and purpled his hair matted close to the skin. I did not know him.

How many of these workers will be taken before their time? They must be made to ready themselves. When I go there now I look around and find myself imagining the faces of the living as though they were already dead their eyes closed or staring wild and blank their faces puffed and white hands locked ready to be put away beneath the earth.

I know too that when I come down to place the tracts again the men will work as before the silence will have lifted. Time slips away from us but we repeat ourselves we walk in the marks of our own footprints we do not awake to see the ending of the world.

19

It rained yesterday and I cried. I have no good explanation for it but I record the matter anyway and perhaps some reason will occur to me later.

I had left my labours and gone outside to find a drizzle setting in with the ground already damp and darkening. I were feeling tired certainly but quite glad for the rain it is an invigorating thing. I took a deep breath of the moist air ready to set off home and then something in my chest turned about like weights balancing and sadness rose up in a wave becoming a sob in my throat causing me to cough from surprise. And then my eyes suddenly streamed with tears and I needed to brush them from my cheeks with the back of my hand the soot and dirt smearing. Then the crying stopped just a strange lingering sadness left behind not severe in any way more like the feeling of a space which that sadness had quickly occupied. Well I were a little ashamed of the episode and not certain what it had arisen from so I were quite glad to think that no one had seen me.

But that were an end to it I have not been bothered by any similar affliction today a good thing too for I have had full employ. I have been to school twice taken the preaching service to Minnard this morning spoke from Samuel 1st Book 2nd Chapter it were a restorative time but the company were small. Our singing voice were meagre it did not do much to lift us from the gloom of the chapel we scratched our way through some well-beloved hymns and I think they were ill-treated by our efforts. I have been on the way to St Germans and changed the tracts and in the evening preached again.

When I came from my lodgings for the evening appoint-
ment I found James waiting outside. My landlady had told
him to wait his shoes were muddy she did not want him
inside but she had not troubled to come and mention to me
that he were there.

I apologized in earnest but he said he had been glad to wait
that the air were fresh and he had not been there long. He
seemed in fine spirits and eager to come hear me preach and
it were good to see him.

We set out together on the road to Landrake. A light drizzle persistent in the air the same as yesterday but not leaving
us too damp. It were a refreshing change to walk to my duties
with the company of a friend the miles seemed shorter I felt a
great energy rise through me as we talked. I were bursting
with heat under my coat and hat I would have removed them
if there had not been the rain and I had not needed my clothes
clean to preach in. James told me stories from his time in the
West and it were a lightening pleasure to listen to him and
allow the concerns of the week to be forgotten. He talked
about the church he attended and spoke well of the work they
did there I think there are places in this land which still thrive
where the Lord's work is more happily done than here. It
renewed my hope a little. His company were very pleasurable it caused me to laugh out loud. It seems of late that I have
not had much cause for laughter.

Spoke that evening the Word of the Lord from The Acts of
the Apostles 2nd Chapter 1st Verse I thought I had spoken it
well and were satisfied that the time were profitably spent.

My Godfather too came up from Burraton to hear me. He
had found a lift on a farmer's wagon so I felt greatly blessed
to have strong friends around me the company seemed much
larger for their presence and they were encouraging in their
comments. Afterwards I waited a short while with the two of
them I knew it were a rare opportunity to be among friends
with no duty to distract me and I were keen to seize it. We sat
on pews at the rear of the chapel grateful for the warmth of

the place and optimistic that the rain would stop it came as a diminishing sound at the windows. It felt quite a cosy little gathering I had a strong sense of companionship there and real happiness in my heart. We talked of many things I cannot recall now what we said except that we came to be discussing the strength of the Body of Christ in our circuit and that James were very eloquent on the matter.

I have come to envy a little his ability to speak of things I find hard. He is quite fluent in his arguments and seems to know the correct words to use when we talk of these matters. I have great trouble because much of what I feel I cannot explain they are mysteries which escape my untutored mind. In my sermons I struggle to get at the truth of things in my heart they seem clear and simple but become greatly confused when I speak of them.

We had spirited argument about the failings of the Church. According to Mr Pendray the body of local preachers across the whole circuit is strong there are over forty of us planned with three more on trial.

So I said that I did not think it were in its preachers that the Church were falling short but in the attitude of the congregations that their spirit were wanting. And it were against that that James argued he said the ideas by which people live are being brought to change that something more than their spirit is at stake that their faith is being turned back to man and to science. And he were insistent on the matter quite passionate in his speech and because it seemed he understood more on this subject than I did I stayed my tongue.

Well it occurs to me now too late what I would have said and this is that we may see many marvels done through science and engineering in this place great bridges built and the railway run but that will not save our souls.

We had precious little time together the night seemed to come down quick and we needed to find our own ways home. Mr Pendray were visiting with a local preacher of the Church Mr Rapson for the night an old friend so when we were done I walked him to that home. My Godfather seemed a frail thing as he stood and needed my hand on his arm to balance him as we moved. I know he is alone and I feel I should do more to care for him after all the kindnesses he has done my family and I love him in Christ but it feels as though I cannot quite make the duty my own. There are times when I feel I have been seared by his kindness that I have a heavy burden of debt to repay him duties which weigh on me like bruises. There are plenty chores already with little enough time to attend to them and I feel I must withhold myself the pleasure of my friend's company. Perhaps when he is gone these labours that have been handed me will be less and the call to stay here not so strong.

He is become such a small man it is strange I have not seen it before. But then he were old when I first knew him and because he is so strong in the Lord I imagine him more fully grown than I am and a bigger man than in truth he is. Now though stiff backed and hunched over for walking his outer coat stretching tight with the curve he is barely half my size. Our progress were painful slow but he were sensitive to my thoughts he understood how our pace frustrated me a little.

I am not so fast as I used to be he said.

We have time I said.

We stopped a moment to rest. My muscles twitched with impatience I do not know why I felt a need to be away I had only my bed to go to.

I grow tired so easily now he said and there were no sign of complaint in his voice. It is strange how we come to slowness at the end of our lives.

You have a few years remaining I am sure I said.

He looked at me.

And will you be getting married? he asked. You are leaving it quite late.

I hesitated. I had not been expecting the conversation and felt uncomfortable to be talking of it.

I do not have the money I said. My life does not allow it the work is too hard now. The Church too needs what I have.

Perhaps you are giving too much he said. I know we are bound to give from our income but perhaps you should look to yourself as well and think about your situation. There are other ways of giving. Your duties for example. I am sure there must be a young woman among one of the congregations who would be glad to have you. Do you not want a family?

I am young yet I said there is time.

But I did not believe it I felt I had forsaken these things that they had passed me by. I knew what he would say that I am near enough to thirty that my father were not much older than me when he were taken that my days are few. And still I feel like a child ignorant of the world not knowing how the years have passed how I have come to this place already a man. A rush of blood came to my head panicking me with the dizziness of years already gone. The future seemed to plunge deep as a chasm before me with nothing to do but fall forward into it and await the hard ground.

A family will suit you he said. You do not see much of your own any more.

And I knew it were true so it did not seem like too much reproach to me. I let him speak.

Would you not want one? he asked. Were you not happy with your parents?

Of course I said. Of course I were.

It seemed then that there were something else he wanted to say to me but did not and fell instead into quiet thought. And I wondered if the reason he did not speak were because it were strange for him a man without a family to be giving me advice on the matter. I do not know why he has had no family I do not know if it were a choice or the result of loss I thought I would wait for the right time to ask him and it were not now.

He started to speak again.

94

I am a little worried for you he said. Then he stopped there just met my eye and did not finish perhaps deciding that the opinion were not for me after all.

Though the truth were I knew his thoughts better than that his meditations were open to me and they seemed to take a morbid bent. He saw me growing old too swiftly he were dwelling on his own death and then mine to follow and he wanted neither of us to go alone into eternity. But I did not wish my Godfather to talk with me about death. I have had enough of the word enough of the thought of it. It has come to feel like a sickness in my body which will possess me even in life. I took his arm and brought him to his door the day ended.

20

The week too were swiftly gone. The days have swung around
to their end and my spirit seems so oppressed. It were uplift-
ing to have had some company in the Lord the class meetings
are so poorly attended it is often enough when I go that I have
just one brother with me or I am there alone. It is a sad state
to see the Church this way and the time to correct these things
is short. But I find that the joy brought to me by these brief
moments with my friends lives just a short while in my heart
it seems that each day new blood flows there which remembers nothing of yesterday. All I have remaining is the residue
of happiness the sense that my joys have been taken and that
they may not come again. And one solemn thought seems to
sink deeper than the rest and that is whether we shall all meet
again doubtless some that have met this week will exchange
worlds before another year rolls round and I have to ask
myself the question Lord is it I?

And this were not my only reason to think on our mortality
and the timing of it for I have heard today that Harriet French
is worse and I fear she is not much longer with us I must find
time to visit her soon.

21

Two more weeks have gone from us and I could not keep them from slipping from me they have already blurred in my mind so that I cannot even say what they contained. We dream our time away I do not know how we will awake from it.

I do not normally parcel out the year into pieces and say that I must get such-and-such a thing done in that time but I have reckoned today that seeing as it is late September then by that yardstick the year is already near three-fourths gone and I have had little time for myself I have been called to work so hard. When I lay down after work I am terribly tired. I bunch the blankets together in my cot and burrow into them. But still my head is full of clamour I hear the ringing of iron and many voices from the day speaking to me again echoing loudly in the back of my skull. So there is no peace nor calm not even as I lay down to sleep.

It is a dispiriting thing to think that another year has almost escaped us with many of the hopes I had for it remaining unfulfilled. I have not been home for nine months and feel the call of family. Yet I have guarded my spare hours carefully and desired to spend that time with those who may be not much longer with us. I trust my family will forgive me the absences they endure as I do my duties. I have not felt free to call the time my own to do as I would if I chose only for myself.

Today is the Sabbath and for the first time in months I have woken with the cold and needed to get up swiftly and move around to keep warm. The day has been spent as follows in the morning I went out to walk I changed the tracts. It rained throughout a sobering chill fastened close to the damp. When the hour came I attended a service in Tideford preached by Brother Cottle the congregation were disappointingly few in number. We had a simple lunch together and then in the afternoon there were a visiting speaker at the chapel hall a man from the Wesleyan Missionary Society who spoke well about the work done by our Church overseas and I contributed to a collection afterwards but found that the poor nations were rather distant from my mind today. We ourselves seem not much better than the poor savages who know nothing of God. I wonder if we are still strong enough to take on this work if the missionaries should not return to preach to us.

I left the meeting soon after it were over and hurried to St Germans. Harr French has been in my thoughts all week it has been terrible to imagine that the poor girl has been suffering while I have been unable to visit and I felt I could not arrive too soon.

William came from the house and met me on my approach it turned out I had been seen coming along the road and he had been sent down by his mother to greet me. His face were fresh with something he wore his smart white shirt the sleeves rolled back though it were not warm. His shoes had wet mud round the soles I could tell he had been out early in the rain. I thought he might have been at chapel in the morning but I had not seen him.

Harriet is sleeping he said. You should not come in.

Then I will not disturb her I said. Is your mother home? I will happily spend some time with her.

She sent me to tell you Harriet is asleep and you could not come in.

Ah she is busy then I said and did not know what else to say to him.

I heard at the chapel your sister is taken worse lately I said.

Aye he said.

I am sorry. Has the doctor been?

I went to fetch him this morning but he could not come.

Well I said. I am not sure he has been of best use in any case. Perhaps she will be better served by prayer. The Lord takes care of *his* own. You have been praying for her?

Aye he said but he paused before he said it and did not look at me. I nodded approval.

But still there were something apparent in his face I did not know what he expected of me. He appeared discomfited and it occurred to me he might think me angry with him because he had not been coming to class. But I did not know how to set him at ease and after we stood a moment in uncomfortable silence I decided to leave. It were a disappointment. I felt a strong need to see Harr then and I did not know when I would have the opportunity to visit again or if that time might come too late.

If you will tell her I came by when she wakes I said. And say to your mother she is in my prayers.

A slight wavering of his chin which I took for assent.

I expect I will see you at school I said to him.

He went inside. I felt gloomy after he had gone. The news did not sound good and it were a poor sign that Harr were not even well enough for visitors. I lingered a moment on the road uncertain what to do then resolved to return home and devote some time to prayer on her behalf.

I took the path beside the cottage. It would take me on a way around the edge of St Germans a pleasant trail I do not often find cause to take. Along the whitewashed wall of the house which becomes ivy-covered at the rear and then past the small garden. There is plenty of colour remaining here there are ferns in frittered green and climbing roses just out of bloom on the south wall of the neighbouring house. I glanced up at the roof above Harr's small window observed some tiles cracked in two and the pattern of the slates ever more complex with newly scored lines a depressing reminder that there were still repairs needing to be done another duty I had neglected. As I looked up I saw movement at the window an outline which I thought were Mrs French and the movement were sudden with a sense of urgency and I felt quite upset that I had not been able to go in and help I were sure I might have been of some use it caused my spirit to feel very low.

I took up walking again heading towards the almshouses the short terrace backed by a row of trees tall chestnuts solid and sheltering. A thrush chattered brightly somewhere. Autumn is close upon us and though the trees are still large in volume wide-girthed and thickly dressed with leaves their green now is almost gone mixed with yellow as it has fallen to the ground a slow rust overtaking the woods. Autumn were always something to look forward to a great season to be a child we would kick up the leaves finding something so rewarding in the simple pleasure of it. It is a shame we cannot stay children for ever and remain blind to the slow death of the land. How different it will all be in a few months the bare trees revealed as dark gnarled bodies. Something inside them though lives through the yearly famine and they always find new colour. I trust it is the same for us all.

I had time spare and should have called in on Mrs Truscott at the almshouses but I had lost my enthusiasm for visiting and were feeling the need to be outside so I walked on past that place and took a path still wet from the rains which led out around the village and in a meandering way took me home to Quethiock. In the kitchen on my return I took care to clean the mud from my shoes and sweep away the dirt I had brought in with me I did not have the heart to face the complaints of my landlady she is mean I think a mean woman.

22

Tomorrow afternoon I am due to preach in Crafthole the text is Matthew 7th Chapter 27th Verse I have made my sermon notes I have them here.

And it fell and great was the fall of it.

How after *he* preached on the mountaintop and made many sayings that *he* might convey *his* wisdom to the mind of the listeners how *he* made even a parable of *his* parables a lesson on how we should hear and obey *his* lessons

1ly   The building of a house it is a very bad one dangerous in the summer season and calm weather and certain to fall by the storms of winter

   1   It has a poor foundation if we look carefully we can read this inscription on it which says DISOBEDIENCE on one side and UNBELIEF on the other

   2   The ground on which it stands is poor the sands of fancy

   3   The material is likewise very inferior

2ly   Its destruction it fell and great were the fall of it

3ly   The lessons we should learn from this text

   1   And first of all let us be careful to have a good foundation

   2   We may be wearied in the building but listen to the voice of the Master and obey *his* Word

3 Let us not fear when the floods come and the
storms blow the ground is firm the rock of ages

4 But let those be assured who will not listen
to the voice of the Master neither obey this
command that soon their house will be shaken
and the stones of the walls fall down upon
them and they will be left exposed to the
tempest without shelter

23

I had a cold start and early too there were no movement from
the town when I went out. Last night I looked to the sky for a
sign of the weather but there were nothing there just a plane
of grey cloud a slippery skin over my head with nothing to be
read from it. I sensed the darkness of early morning to be full
of expectation for the coming of day with all our movements
still awaiting their order and the hours yet to be assigned. I
felt I could still hope for something good.

There were no shelter to be had from the hedgerows the
lanes were become channels for cold air. I had a strong wind
at my back it swept the leaves before me they tumbled as if
running downhill it looked like the land moved beneath my
feet. The path bore me on the leaves skipped and raced.

By rights today I should have had a horse for the journey
but there has been some disagreement with the farmer that
owns him it seems that the last time he loaned the beast to the
Church it had come back lame and he says he is disinclined to
further charity. I have heard though from other sources that
the problem were that it had been badly shod at that farmer's
local smithy. And I were tired of troubles and argument and
the work that would be needed to fetch one so I thought it
would be easier to walk the distance I have done it before.

Out from Quethiock the road swings south-west to
Menheniot and I followed it a while. In the half-dark I came
into the trees through a dry-stone wall by a gate held between
stone posts. There are firs and pines there new woods which
are quick to grow the treacle scent of them sweet in the air.
From beneath the cool trees I came out up to the Tiddy crossing it by the bridge near Menheniot. Then I left the road to
head south through the valley it is a beautiful place wooded

and unfarmed. Straggled heronries perch high in the branches there. Went through a meadow thick with ferns rusted like iron and up to a road again the last few miles ahead of me over barer folds of land. The path cuts through the turf running like a trough or trench across the heath with small levees of earth on either side.

But I did not give my way much thought my mind were bent in on itself on past days which came vividly to me. The even pace of my legs seemed to move my mind and conjured strong memories of my first visit to Crafthole when I were seven or eight years old a memory so clear I were almost transported into it. Returned to a Sabbath in late July a clear perfect day with a breeze beckoning me to the sea. I remember being awake by five or half past in the morning when my father came in to rouse me. His pain in those days were not sufficient to keep him home he still travelled to preach. I were too small to walk such a long way and the distance between St Eve and Crafthole is greater than the one I have had today so we strode together as far as St Germans and collected a horse from the chapel stable.

There were the railway of course but my father did not think it fit for the Sabbath it requires workers and he believed they should have more respect for their Lord than to labour that day. A train came by when we were in sight of the line and I craned my neck to look at it though my father ignored the sight I know he prayed for the souls of those using it. Well I have failed him in this because there are days since when I have suffered their labours because I have had need of the service and if they aid the Lord's work then perhaps there is some good come of it.

On the horse I sat proudly in front of him my eyes open to everything. The journey a blur of colour a melding of many places new to me it were the furthest then that I had travelled from home. My father indicated the farms as we passed them an invocation of names which I whispered to myself the whole journey long and find I can still recite now: *Trehunist Trenance Goodmerry Leigh Furslow Dannett Penpoll Haye.*

The farmland fell behind us and the land changed we came onto the cliff and I first saw the sea it were a beautiful thing a fine living cloth spread out to the horizon. I could not believe it were so vast. A deep shifting blue richer than the sky. The smell of salt so keen I could taste it on my tongue. The sight awed me furnished a view which has burned in my memory these years. It felt as though the scene had been waiting for me a long time.

My father preached at the cliff-top chapel before a gathering of people from the village. I accompanied him to read the lesson we prepared it together beforehand he wanted to show that I could read and thus demonstrate his pride in me. All week long I had practised it in a loud voice my mother telling me to slow down always to read slower than I wished to. When we were done some of the men shook my hand and told me I had read well asked where did I learn but I were too shy to talk to them. I stood quietly by waiting for my father wondering if he would stay all day by the door exchanging greetings.

But he did not. And in the afternoon we followed a steep path down the grassy cliff and walked together along the beach. When I went down to the water I approached it slowly not knowing how it would feel not knowing if it would welcome me if were a transgression to touch something so wonderful. We walked along the fringe of the waves and it felt as though my life were suddenly made open I ran on the sand experienced for the first time its soft give. Behind me ragged curves the tracks of my broken footprints. We passed beachcombers collecting wood two limpet pickers sitting beneath the cliff they were old women and I remember how happy I thought they seemed. I were too young then to notice the raggedness of their clothes or to imagine that their warm wrinkled faces were so shaped by hard lives. All I felt in the day were freedom.

We walked along onto an eroded slate bed a dark slab slanting out into the sea. The sun glaring brightly. I squinted my eyes. Felt open to the elements there exposed to the sun crushed beneath its heat against that rock as though I were splayed on an anvil beaten by the hammer and the light. I walked out as far as I could before the grey rock grew black and slippery and the waves threatened to soak my breeches.

On our return we veered towards the cliff and found a seam of limestone where the drip of water created a grotto of pools. I have learned since that those cascades which seem to be rock though green and pink are properly called calcite. My father told me that long ago the pools were thought to have healing power. It seems that people once looked to the land for healing as though they knew God were in it. We come to know our Lord through what we see of the world but only if the change is inside do we feel *him* there is a leap of reason and faith to be made and it is a wide chasm we must cross but then how happy and blessed are we to know *him*.

Still on the beach on that day in my youth I am dressed in my church clothes and though I have taken care in playing the hems of my breeches are wet and grown heavy with sand. We walk down to the pebbled shore and wash our hands the water is refreshing so cold that it makes me shout and laugh and my father laughs too at my surprise a rare sound and loud which conjures an unspeakable happiness within me but it comes from near twenty year past and I cannot hear it any longer.

My memories of that day greatly quickened the road and carried the miles swiftly from me. I only wished that today were as fine as it had been then but as I neared the coast it did not seem that we would be so blessed. There were a fiery dawn the sky coloured red like the clay of the soil a beautiful sight but a poor sign.

As I climbed up to the cliff edge I felt a great pull. It were a wonderful scene awaiting me I am always glad when my journeys bring me there. The great space of air and water opening out a breeze which fills my lungs even if the day is still. The sea has a gravity to it. It draws and sucks on the land. Over the lip of the cliff it seemed close by though there were still real distance to it the path down to the beach is long and steep. But the ocean crash were loud. A thousand waves peaked briefly and each in turn were gone flecks of light showing white against the turbid blue. I came tired and a little hungry along the edge open to the wind stepping through thick turf among patches of gorse and came finally to my destination.

Crafthole chapel is a small place up above the village tucked into a plait in the land. There were an older church here which were taken down near on a hundred years ago. This one we have now is rebuilt from the old moorstones by the Wesleyan community here in the days of revival in my grandfather's time and both he and my father have preached here before me. I cannot fully communicate the strange assurance I feel from knowing that my ways have been patterned with my ancestors' footsteps. The chapel here feels a safe place a secure haven of stone quite removed from the wildness beyond its walls.

On either side the low door there are small windows of glass the unadorned panes stained simply with red and green. The roof is slate set at a low angle for protection from onshore gales. On the cliff-facing side there are no windows just full stones and little light reaches inside. A wind-bent tamarisk curls for shelter by the wall.

There are few windows then but it is kept well-stocked with candles there were ranks of them already lit when I arrived. The steward had been up early to prepare the place to unbolt the shutters and open the Bible at today's lesson. He were waiting inside glad that I had arrived in good time anxious to instruct me. I have met him before he is a fussy man given to more preparation than I would have bother with he chattered endlessly while unlocking the vestry for me but I did not listen to him much. I breathed the air felt my skin to be prickled by the good atmosphere in the chapel. And allowed my mind to wander. It occurred to me then that I had quite forgotten the steward's name and he did not introduce himself again so I trust I were polite to him.

Inside with the candle-dry warmth and dusty air it feels something like a stable a place for animals to shelter. Well perhaps it is not far from the truth we are all animals sleeping in the dark houses of the Lord not fit for true light. The candles fretted made darting shadows as though there were creatures moving along illumined walls at the edge of my vision hiding in the corners embracing the darkness but still eager to eaves-drop on the Word. I felt I could follow the movement of the light as though it were a body a bulky flickering in the space bright at its centre and orange at the extreme. There were some quality to it that felt heavenly. My sight grainy and imperfect and something of sleep in the air. The pews beck-oned me seemed like a bier or bed where I might lie down and rest.

I sat quietly on a chair in the vestry to pray but felt half-called to sleep so stood again waiting to be summoned to preach and stretched my legs which were stiffening after the walk.

24

The chapel were near empty for the morning service. There were one old lady who sat at the furthest pew from the pulpit she stood silent and unmoving during the hymns. The only voice I heard raised were my own. Our afternoon meeting then were not until three and the intervening hours slow I waited with the steward and listened to him enumerate his cares. I found I did not greatly take to the man. Then when the hour finally came I were again to be disappointed with the congregation just two others apart from us it is a long way to come to see such little reward. There were no sign of the men who had greeted me when I were a child. I wondered where they had gone now well I know there are many who have chosen to work on the Sabbath feeling they must provide for their families not trusting the Lord to do so. I were deeply saddened and made to think how this church were once raised on hope alone how people came to be close to Heaven and saved of their sins. Seems there is little faith remaining.

I preached from my notes felt no voice fill me just the hard unbending Word of God which I dragged from the page and let turn on my own tongue.

It were an empty sermon which could not have provided them much satisfaction and they must return to their homes still hungry. And afterwards there were no food neither so our bellies were empty too just the same as our hearts. The steward apologized to me as though it were a small thing he said that a storm were coming and we must leave quickly for home. Hinted that the congregations now were too small to warrant feeding. Well it seemed an unnecessary meanness I felt ill-treated I did not think it would have required much work to have brought something for the preacher and surely a small crowd were easier to provide for than a large one. I had brought nothing with me and if the weather were turning I would not have time to go with someone to the village and wait in their kitchen while they begrudged me a small share of their own food.

It were darkening when we left the church the clouds already coloured like quarry slate after rain. The wind had got up it felt cold on the cliff. The billowing sky blew in a great turmoil so much so it looked like a rushing ocean went above. It appeared like it would rain and I knew I had better soon leave. Not a day to walk on the beach the tide were high and pressing.

The waves far beneath caught my eye they crashed white on black rocks a beautiful sight churning away but it seemed to threaten it were not like the morning. There were a contest between sea and these limestone cliffs and today it looked sure the sea would win it will still beat on the land when these rocks are worn away and we are gone before.

I helped fasten the shutters over the windows of the chapel it seemed we were preparing for a storm like the wise man in the parable but I did not think that this church built on rock served much purpose if no one came to it. We barred the wood door shut closed the chapel tightly no doubt it will lie empty and unused for another week.

The steward then were swiftly gone trotting off down the path so I exchanged a few words with the couple that had come they were a Mr Blake and his wife. He has been a fisherman in these waters for many years is an old man now the days when he took out his boat are long gone. His face were tanned skin all shrivelled and beneath his hat there were signs of unruly hair strong and thick as cord and white as salt. His wife it transpired is half-deaf well I had spoken my sermon loudly enough with a confidence I did not feel but I do not think she heard much of it. Perhaps her heart were more attuned to our Lord's voice than her ears and it were better that way. I hope I did not drown the Good Word out.

We were happy to see a young preacher she said. It is always old men and you would think we have enough of them.

A slow smile on her husband's face.

I am not so young any more I said leaning forward to her better ear.

Come now she said. All these old fellows saying the same things every week in a different chapel. It makes me quite glad I can't hear them. My ears may be going but my mind is not yet ready to put up with nonsense. I have half a mind to get up there myself I'd have a few things to say.

And why not I said.

But she had turned to look at her husband and not seen me speak it seemed much of her ability to hear were by her sight.

How are your legs? she asked him. Are you ready to go now? His legs are bad she said to me.

Her husband there still smiling. A slight shake of his head which may have been an answer. Something in his eye I thought. But he were quiet. It is the same with many of the fishermen I have known. They are accustomed to solitude on their boats and even if the world were ending about them they could abide with patience until it were their time. They have waited for the earth so why not for Heaven too. Still something in his eye kept me though I listened to the woman and answered I could not stop watching his face.

She saw me looking.

Don't you mind Joshua she said. Sometimes he is still half out to sea.

The slow smile spread a little.

And I felt that it were not for her but for me. He smiled at me with something shining some memory or thought that came with clouds and water in his mind and old sunlight behind them breaking through. I saw the ocean swimming in his eyes and then suddenly I were afraid again afraid for age and passing for being claimed by loss enveloped in its mystery. We have no freedom. If I live as old as him I will wither similarly I will grow weak and look hazy eyed and broken to my youth and will not even have the comforts that are afforded him a wife a home and the sea in his eyes. I thought then that I would die alone.

He were watching me. The fear shook in my spine a little. I felt that I were tired that these dark thoughts came upon me more easily when my body were weak.

A good sermon he said he shook my hand. A tough grip more iron than muscle. My arm trembled. He held my eye. His wife fussed beside him straightening his coat.

Then the two of them thanked me for coming and bade me a fair journey though I saw them look to the sky and knew they thought of their own walk home. Well I smiled at their concern not begrudging them their rest but we could almost see the houses of Crafthole from where we stood it were not at all far and downhill all the way so even if their pace were slow they would be warm in their home before I had barely begun.

25

I left by the cliff path it were perhaps not the quickest way but I desired to see for as long as I could the ocean and I knew too that if it rained it would be less muddy than the track through the fields. I thought the sea air might do me some good. The clouds gathered in layers from the west piling upon each other until it seemed the air could not bear the weight of them. Yet it did not rain. The sky seemed to go black as wet ash it came from over the sea like ink spilled and blooming there. Thick marram blew with the wind in ripples grey in the light and I went on through up along the narrow path. The wind came over the cliff so I were not afraid to be blown over it the updraft were so fierce it might have lifted me up and placed me back on the road. Such miracles are not unknown. As I walked I offered a swift prayer for a safe journey I felt a long way from home. Then the first spray of rain.

In Quethiock some days you can smell the sea and the salt brought by a strong wind from the south but it is not like it is here where every breath feels like it expands inside filling me more than the air I am used to. It seemed like it would push stale air from the very depths of my lungs and were an exhilarating sensation. I grew sad thinking on how precious my time were if I had more of it I would come to walk here more often.

But I felt better again for walking letting the fear be trodden out by my feet into the forgiving earth. Felt good enough to raise my head from the course of my step. I saw shearwaters over the sea knew them by their rigid wings they glided as though on canvas sails. There were white gulls making use of the wind to soar from the cliffs dark spots of black at their wingtips. They were lifted on the air higher than my eye could follow their harsh call blew all around warning of the storm it almost caused me to stop it might have been a human cry for help. I think there were fulmars perched on the rocky ledges already sheltering in their feathers bundled white beneath silver-grey. It is a very great wonder how God provides for *his* creatures.

The cliff way is not easy it goes down to the bay then up over the headland before I could leave it again to the north. It were a steep climb and my legs felt strained with the effort. The path at some places were grown over with thorny gorse and I must push through it I felt the barbs prick my skin coming through my trouser cloth. By the time I got back up above the sea again the rain started it came in heavy drops with each drop near a handful burst of water. Gusts forced me back and made me stumble. Well I am a big man built strong from my labours and not easily pushed about but I were nothing compared to the force there. I wrapped my coat around me and drew breath. Steadied my feet. Echoing in the air were the distant boom of water in a blow-hole an uneven beat against the screeching wind. I would have liked to have seen it but I had not the time.

I should have turned inland then but I stayed awhile in the last of the light to watch the sea. To be a sailor there in such a storm would teach even a man without faith how to pray. The water seemed to boil from beneath it swelled upwards and pushed the waves energetically against the land. And then I thought my rain-blurred eyes played tricks on me for I saw the sea rise from the centre of its boiling pulled up to Heaven by a point rising to meet the clouds it rose and formed in a single pillar like stone. But this column were not straight neither solid it twisted and bent in the centre where it grew thin it danced around in a massive design but slow and blind. I saw it through squalls of rain and each time I lost it I thought it had been an illusion but then the squall would pass and still it stood. There were a roar in the air far off a low keening almost below my ability to hear it.

The sight I am sure were a waterspout I have met sailors before who have seen them and have heard talk so I knew what it were but I never thought in my life I would see one. The perspective were very confusing to judge I think it were a long way out to sea so that means it were of great size. I have seen nothing like it in Nature the water made into a living thing the drops come together into a being as we are drawn from dust and blood. It seemed to me like some kind of sign reminded me of the Bible where it says God guided the Israelites as they fled Egypt and it showed me that the miracles *he* works through Nature are beyond our grasp. *And the Lord went before them by day in a pillar of cloud to lead them the way.* And then the sky ducked low and embraced me and I lost my view for good.

My coat were thick with water I did not notice until I started walking again. I would have stayed on the headland longer but the rain grew dense and then hardened so I could not see even the edge of the cliff beside me and it were no longer so safe. It were soon dark. It is strange to think that God performs these wonders though none can see it and I gave thanks that *he* had accorded me this view of *his* work. Only I did not know what the sign intended and I asked *him* to show me but there were no lightning flash then no voice coming to interpret it for me.

The way home were still many miles and I were soaked through half thinking to turn around and find a place at Crafthole but I needed to return for work and knew there were no guarantee the storm would not continue the next day.

The wind were kinder away from the cliff came in with a diminishing shriek the rain less painful and driven anyway into my back I no longer had to fight against it. More sheltered now I cleared my eyes wiping away the water as it streamed down my face. Saw in the lapsed light the reach of ferns beneath the rise. Blackened earth beneath my feet softening with the rain. It made a still sound falling. I felt an imbalance to walk on the soft turf my body heavy but my feet light not feeling the ground. I felt a chill and swung my arms but it did little except soak me further. My clothes were heavy on me. The darkness fell about and I knew it would be a long cold time before I would be home.

I were so wrapped up in my thoughts trying to keep from thinking of the cold that I did not see someone come towards me until they were right alongside a crookbacked figure wrapped in a black cloak walking slow in the centre of the path. I started and jumped to the side but they did not flinch just went by me in slow steps perhaps they too were sheltering deep within their frame and never saw me at all. There were a basket on the figure's back hanging from a strap which ran around its forehead. I caught a glimpse of the face beneath the hood it were only an old fishwife heading home from some chore inland a black dress evident beneath the cape. She were ancient her face wrinkled downwards to a hard sharp chin lips fluttering around unheard words. Eyelids half-closed by age. It were a strange sight something unreal about her being there. I cannot even say now if I saw all this or have summoned the details in remembering perhaps because it were too dark for me to have seen everything I now recall but this is how the face comes to me and I have no other guide. Then she were gone into the veil of rain with no sound and something lacking in my sense of the encounter so that it seemed I might have imagined it. I stood still a moment before remembering where I were and the path ahead and I began walking again.

The miles passed beneath me they were hard won and the rain did not relent. I were blown about by the wind it were rough going and quite slow. My legs began to ache sharp pains shooting down behind my knees the left worse than the right forcing me into a limp lengthening my journey further.

In time I came back onto the high ground found the moor rising away to the west. At least I felt as though I were back in more familiar land and though I were ragged and beaten down by the clawing damp a feeling of belonging rose in me. I looked up from the path to the shrouded hills and felt as clear as my heart something call to me as though I had some old home there on the moor. It is not the first time I have felt something beckon me here it comes often when I am out walking at odd hours. As though the cold clutch of the land had something of me already in it.

That ache of belonging stayed with me a long way it were not washed out by the rain. I chose the quicker route not detouring towards Menheniot as I had come I wished to be soon out of the wet. Decided to follow the path as far as I were able and come over the Tiddy by the ford it would save me some time. The pain in my legs were worsening and I had some concern about the distance. The rain still fell unremitting.

But I quickly came to regret not choosing the road for the path grew thick with mud and I were hampered by having to stay on the edge of it. I trod slowly over the thick-grassed road edge it were uneven ground. Often enough I tripped as though the grass grew up into knotted traps and once cut my hand on the bushes as I caught myself my progress were painful slow.

The first sign that I were nearly at the ford were the widening path but I knew the river were in torrent long before I reached it the rushing sound were heavy. And it were worse than I thought. The Tiddy is a tame river in summer made of quiet stretches and slow pools of sleeping trout. No rapids just a gentle babbling over rocks where the course steepens. So what I saw then made me think I had lost my way in the dark it could hardly be the same water. The ford is rarely dry but I have never seen it rise much above the height of my ankles I could not be sure of the gauge now but reckoned it would reach my waist and it seemed to flow too swift to wade safely. There were power there in the fast churning a thundering sound of water turning over and falling hard on itself. I did not think I could cross. I looked upstream knowing I would have to decide which way to go hopeful for a narrowing point or a fallen tree.

Up from the ford I thought I saw someone across on the opposite bank a short distance upstream. I did not know whether my eyes saw true in the dark and rain but it seemed like a figure. So that were the second time on the walk and I wondered if there had been sent devils to worry me or angels to watch me or if they were just shadows in my mind distorted by the storm. But this time I were sure it were a man perhaps someone come out to fish. Well the fishing is good enough here but it were a foolish time for it the river so swollen and the rain in sheets. So I thought perhaps it were someone like myself cut off and looking for a way across. I called up to them but the noise of the river drowned my call and then I had lost sight of them.

I kept on along the river through the mud and trees often being forced a little way in from the course by thick bushes and fighting my way back to the water. At a bend the river widened and smoothed and I stopped to judge if I could swim. And on the far side I saw them again. A thin figure not very big and I thought for some reason that it were William. Well as clear as my memory is now I might just as well have seen a young elm tree I am so unsure of myself. I remember thinking it were him and feeling quite astonished at it but I did not see him clearly. Our eyes are adjusted to familiar patterns and often choose to paint them over the unfamiliar I have been mistaken in this way many times so who can say? But that feeling of recognition persisted.

I had gone some way up the river and the undergrowth were thickening. Further up the flow seemed every bit as fierce and there were nothing to suggest that I would find a much better place to cross. I knew it would be wiser to turn around and find the road again but I could not face the long haul of it. So I thought I would try to cross and if it seemed too strong then I would have no choice but to turn back.

I went down to the edge. The water a cool pressure in front

of me you feel it in the air. Holding the bank I stepped in slipping a little as I swung forward and plunged much further downward than I expected went straight up to my thighs. I felt the press of current forceful against my legs but my feet held the bed so I let go with my hands and took two steps away. It deepened almost to my waist the surface churning enough to splash my face. I felt the cold force and the threat of it. But I had some faith in my own strength too and waded forward leaning into the current my feet finding rocks to push against. The water up to my chest. I half-swum a step further. Wiped the froth from my face and looked to see if my strange companion were still there watching me I saw him there close to the bank. I felt I were past the worst of it past the centre but had forgotten the bend of the river and that the current were strongest on the outside of the bend close to the far bank and when I stepped into its run it hit me with renewed force pushing away at my balance.

I felt my feet begin to slip from under me lost my position against the water and were dragged a little downstream scrabbling for a hold. I could not go forward. I panicked a little looked up desperately to the bank and shouted for help.

Hand me a stick I called. Help me.

I felt that someone were still there but they did not come down to the edge or approach where I could see them.

Help me. Please help me I called.

I reached out with my arms in supplication. And then my feet slipped straight out and I went underwater nearly swallowed a deep draught with the shock. The river swept me quickly along and I were rolled by the churning water so that I lost my sense of which were *up* and which *down* there were no light just black water and somewhere above it black sky it took a long moment to find the surface and when I did and my head broke clear I grabbed just a single breath before I went under again.

My clothes were too heavy they held me under the surface I could not get my arms free. My lungs ached they had not the time to prepare it were all I could do to seal my mouth to quell the urge I had to breathe. I found some strength in my legs to kick against the current and upwards but I were turned and struck against the rocky bed.

But I had luck in that because my feet found the bottom as I turned and pushed out in the right direction and took me through out of the current and struggling against the drag of my clothes I found my feet and pushed until I could grab the bank. I hung there a while. Tried to pull myself up but my arms failed me. Then tried to crawl it but slithered and slipped in the mud and were nearly carried back into the water. I squeezed the handful of grass felt the root tearing but it held and I hung there breathed deep trying to get some strength. Again I felt that there were someone close by that they had followed me along the river to watch my progress but they did not lend a hand.

And one last time I dragged myself up the muddy bank but when I reached land and thought they might finally come over to help me they did not come. It seemed as though they had stayed until they were satisfied I had made it safely and then they had gone.

I had no strength. Nothing left in me to lift me from where I lay slung like a dead animal on the slick riverbank a sheaf of wet grass grasped in my hand. My legs were gone weak as brittle sticks in the end. I felt defeated by the crossing and foolish in defeat if battles were so easily lost and a strong body turned so quickly to weakness then what chance did my soul have? I had thought my body stronger. I cried out in the dark failing even to get a word just a sob coughed from me tears in my eyes. An inner pain rising absorbed by some stupid feeling of pity. I knew I were terrible cold but did not shiver felt it a bad sign but still did not rouse myself. I longed to close my eyes.

I felt a blackness inside the sense of something vast dying. The pain left me. My legs were ice with sharp edges to the numbness. My heart were ash and I a hollow cave it had burned in. And then a spark lit in that ash a small fire I wanted to sleep beside. I lay down it felt clean and a surface like cool flat mud beneath me but my eyes were open I seemed to hover somewhere behind myself pulling away from the body within the body and I watched myself. The bitter smell of smoke all around. There were warmth from the fire I felt it in my shoulders and at the back of my neck I heard voices sound there in popping noises I heard my name called.

It roused me to hear my name. I got up. Staggered over in the dark and felt my way to lean against a tree. The shivering began then I thought it would pull me apart in its violence but I were grateful for it I were shaken back into myself. The rain seemed to have lessened or the trees provided more shelter. There were no one near by nor any sign that there had been.

I had lost my way in crossing the river but I knew I must head away from the sound of the water and so that which had nearly killed me could act for a while as my guide. Still I have never felt so lost. A first heavy leg went forward the knee shocked into searing pain. The other dragged behind it I do not know how I were able to move I had reached something hard within me some kernel that did not break beneath the crushing weight. I am not even sure it were part of me.

I came through the woods the yards falling gradually behind me. But it were deep and dark and I stumbled through branches my face were repeatedly cut by thorns. I did not know I had kept to one direction until the branches came less often and the trees were thinning.

And then a stone wall to climb painfully and over it the road and finally I knew the way. My wet trousers sodden and cold dragging raw on my skin weighing upon the ache in my knees. The hard pressed ground jarring my bones at every step. But I had given my body over to whatever possessed me and it pushed each leg forward not thinking of the pain. I curled exhausted inside my own skull not even seeing the way I remember nothing of the last miles until I looked up and found myself on a road no longer hostile. Quethiock cross ahead of me standing cold and insensible to the night. The rain had ceased I do not know how long ago I had not been aware of it. There were no lights in the houses so I knew I were far into the next morning.

I were still sodden when I came to the door heavy with mud and water dripping. I took off my clothes while still outside my hands were raw with cold too numb for the buttons unable to undress myself. My shirt peeled from me like a heavy layer of my own flesh coming away the way you strip skin from a fish. When I bent down to remove my shoes my legs screamed protest. I went naked into the kitchen took some bread from the side couldn't close my hands around it had to hold it between my fists and push it between chattering teeth. I took the kettle and found it to contain cold dregs of milk I drank it down.

In my room I collapsed beneath the blankets shivering fiercely the bed shaking the whole world shimmering with fatigue. The only warmth a fiery burning at my knees. I slept cold and my dreams were dark I struggled for air in the night woke twice clawing for breath before my nerves calmed and I found some warmth.

26

My landlady woke me early calling my name when I were
still sore from the journey I had slept so deeply that the short
night were quickly gone and the tiredness lay unbroken in
my bones. I thought I must be late for my work but it were
still early I wondered what grievance she had with me that
it troubled her at this time. I wondered if I had left mud the
night before. Well what of it. I have always been diligent in
care yet she has not spoken to me for weeks save to mutter
or complain and again she stood at the door with blame on
her face as though to chide me for chores undone. I looked
out from beneath the blanket. She must have seen how
exhausted I were. Yet she would almost not speak so tight
were her features.

A man came by for you last night she said.

I nodded Oh yes I said.

It were strange to find a voice there and still my own it felt
as though I might have lost it yesterday somewhere on the
path.

She crossed herself as the Catholics are accustomed to do it
is an affectation I detest. As though the gesture could imprint
Christ's love across a heart that did not already know it. I
could not endure her that moment. For she has no true
hunger for the Lord nor respect for the Cross it is as base
superstition with her. But still I needed abide her while I
waited for her to speak.

It were a Mr Haddy I think. He waited some while for you
but then the weather were worsening and he had to leave. He
said he had a message for you.

I knew Mr Haddy he were a steward by the church at St
Germans a good man I thought. He did not often come to

Quethiock his family were further east in Burraton I were surprised that he knew where I lived and more that he had come so far west. He had travelled a long way in the rain to call for me I wondered if Mr Pendray were ill. But something prevented me from asking so still I needed to wait and read nothing of the substance of the word he had brought for me her face were bare of all. I felt a pang of hunger reminding me I had not eaten.

It were to tell you that someone is died yesterday she said a young girl Harriet French God rest her soul.

She crossed herself a second time a brief glimpse of horror in her eyes but it passed in an instant and she were thoughtful again.

I think I knew her mother she added. This were a Mrs French from St Germans?

I could not speak.

She looked to say more but then turned away to go. And then turned again as if to speak but said nothing. And then she left.

I were sick that day with a fever and pain in my legs I could not get out of bed. In the evening my landlady returned to bring me some cold food just left it there on the side with little sympathy asking what I were going to do about work. I ate and slept and do not remember anything else.

27

The week since then has passed in grief and agony. In the days I were busy with work my labours kept me in the dim forge with not much brightness reaching my sight only the fire's glow. It feels as though it has burned a mark into my vision I still see it when I close my eyes an orange smudge persistent to the right stealing any last chance I had to escape into black and cold. My hammer hardly left my hand we had horses to shoe and tools to sharpen there were not much time for rest it has left me aching and weary. I feel the Good Word to be true in this *I have seen the travail which God hath given to the sons of men to be exercised in it*. Mr Coad though were understanding about my illness he did not punish me for missing a day and were sensitive to my weakened state he did not overwork me. I were most grateful.

Wednesday before work I changed the tracts. Took a new packet and went down to the quay. Walking has not been easy this week I have nursed a lameness and a stiffened back so am gone slower than before. The tide were low not much more than a muddy pool there were ketches moored in the residue making their slow rise and fall. A single barge that had not made the previous day's tide sat stranded at an angle in the mud bed waiting for the returning deep.

I did not come into town but went down along the Tiddy beneath the viaduct and something in the low arch of stone drew me up into it. I stood for a long time and stared at it above me. In days past I might have called out to hear my voice echo back but the childish magic of the trick seemed far away.

Thursday I were alone again at the prayer meeting just the Lord and I there I felt *his* pain that there were none to share with *him* and I must make my prayers alone. But it were difficult to concentrate I found my thoughts led to wonder on many things. I did not make profitable use of the time.

The Sabbath came around and Brother Cottle had a fever so I took on his duties he were planned to preach twice. I feel ashamed by the littleness of love I had for it. There were something like disgust or distaste in me afterwards as though every word I had spoken were a lie which poisoned me even as I spat it out. The Spirit were not with me its absence were all I could think of I wonder if the congregation knew it. After the sermon I were deeply ashamed I did not stay long among the parishioners but returned quickly home.

Then the week were past full of horror and so soon gone.

And at every moment of it at every second of every long hour I have known an unspeakable pressure writhing in me. There are questions I have needed an answer to they have burned in every part of my body and I have never felt such disquiet. How did it end for her? Were it a panicked death full of desperation and misery for the family? These questions have caused my whole frame to tense but the frustration could not squeeze from me. I needed to have been there. I have needed to know did she feel her Master with her or go crying and afraid?

Well I have heard today from Dr Coryton and he said that it were a good death that she did not suffer greatly but received her call peacefully that she held on to her faith and were ushered gently into the darkness there to await the renewal of the Light.

28

It has been Harvest at the chapel it has fallen late this year and feels to be a subdued festival. Because the children came to participate with the adults in the service proper I were excused my class duties. They brought gifts of fruit and vegetables to carry to the front when the minister called and tomorrow they will be sent out to distribute them among the parish. Even with seven or eight schoolers present we were not many in number I have sung loudly to try and get our spirits up and let joyful noise fill the place. It should be a blessed time of thanksgiving and praise but I did not feel it. The smell of straw and apples though created a pleasing atmosphere in the chapel returning it to feel more a part of the land too often it seems to be separate from it.

William were absent. Well I hoped in my heart he had gone with his mother to the Quaker meeting because it seemed that he would be in need of Christian fellowship during this difficult time but I did not have much reason to be optimistic about the truth of it.

After the service I kept a small box of vegetables aside to deliver to Mrs French they would get nothing otherwise and when my responsibilities at the church were complete I took them to her.

She came herself to answer the door. Held on to the frame of it for support as she did so. William hovered at her shoulder standing protectively beside her close enough to be able to assist her if she required it the terrible frailty of grief were evident in her. It almost brought me to tears to see it but I have not yet been able to cry. Sorrow comes in bursts it rises up and moistens my eyes and then leaves it will not set in.

I am sorry I said. I held the box forward and William came to take it from me he placed it on the floor behind him.

Well. Thank you. It is good of you to come. There were not many at the funeral we did not see you.

I could not escape work. I had wanted to come.

No matter. It is kind of you to come now.

She were . . . She will be with her Master now I said I stumbled the words.

We were always appreciative of your visits she said. She was happy for company and grateful to the chapel that you could spare so much of your time.

It were nothing I said.

William had his hand on his mother's shoulder seemed to pull her back softly into the house. She looked exhausted. There were no change in her bodily shape since I had seen her last but something about her whole *being* appeared emaciated as though she had been worn down by loss to nothing but voice and shadow the two elements bound together by anguish.

I am so sorry I said. I really cannot say.

Then I apologized for the intrusion and said a hurried goodbye promised only that I would visit again at an easier time and that they need only ask if there were anything they required. And though it were a hard duty dispensed with one I had not looked forward to at all I have felt no relief that it is over.

While our spirits have felt the storms of late the weather has somehow continued fine. Feels to be a curious aberrance. Among patches of moorland heather there is still some late colour they call me *home* and there is something cheering even in the mention of the word. I miss very much being surrounded by my family their presence seemed to assure that sense of purpose I have of late been lacking. And now my visit is finally done with it feels like I am released again to go there. I shall wait for my next free day. Until then no day will be so hard as today it is as though every small part of it has been set aside to be a reminder of them. The view from the chapel akin to the spots we used to play in. Steep woods surrounding the farm the gullies entering them turning to mud in autumn rain. And the festival were a diminishing echo of how it has been in years past. It seemed lesser now even though it is a smaller chapel there in St Eve for that place were packed full. My brothers and I would squeeze onto a pew a box of fresh-dug potatoes or similar on our laps their smell mixing with the earth that still clung to them. Our mother beside us her voice full of rising.

If the season had been kind and we had been successful on the farm much of our work were already done the grain crimped and stored. Harvest marked a rare day of good food for us my eldest brother John would take a pig and bleed it then scald it over the trough with water boiled on the fire. I wonder if they will do that today though it will not be John he is in Australia. Last year we only had one pig so perhaps they have kept it. I miss the cats running about we kept them wild it does not do to domesticate them overmuch but sometimes on a night the old tom grown soft and slow with age would come looking for friendly attention. My memories are strangely sweet for I were worked hard as a boy and young man both but I think they were joyful times none the less.

Sometimes in those happy days I imagined how *his* harvest would be. How *his* workers would come among fertile fields of corn grown taller and more golden than any I have seen in these farmlands the corn swaying from its own swollen weight. And though they come through the field unseen the corn falls as though scythed by an immaculate blade the grain landing to one side and the chaff to the other. It were always a pleasing idea more than once I were moved to use it for an illustration in my sermons I would invite the congregation to imagine such a sight and call them to its glory. There were farmers among them who responded to such devices. But the story does not seem to have its hold any longer I am afraid *his* fields may be left unharvested and the crop to dry and wither and that all the good grain will be blown to the winds and lost.

Now the week is gone too and I cannot recall it I have not felt much purpose to events. Found myself at times forgetful of what I were in the middle of doing as though something in the world had changed and I could not see the result but were waiting to be told what were new and what were now required. I have written a letter to my mother and while writing I thought on the value of a good home.

I am hopeful though that I will experience such circumstances again. I think so much of my own unhappiness emanates from the unpleasantness in my lodgings. I feel unwelcome here it affects my day it gnaws on my faith it infects me I think and no wonder I find it hard to keep a right mind on my duties as they come around.

So I am feeling a little sick with longing for home and have tried to reassure myself with the promises made to us that in the end we will have our belonging. For our Lord Jesus has said that he goes to prepare a place for us *In my Father's house are many mansions: if it were not so I would have told you*. And it is a sweet promise quite uncomplicated a clear and kind thing to leave with us.

Because I have not found the time lately I wrote to Mr Pendray too though I managed only a short note. I sent him all my wishes though I feel bad in my heart because I should have gone to visit him. I found the act of writing to be tiring I do not have a mind for the activity and my eyes have come to aching feeling distended in their sockets. But I were not done with it yet I have had preparation work for my sermon to fill the remainder of the evening. I were slow at forming my notes it kept me up late.

29

The days still come. Feels as though they should cease to pass but death does not trouble them they arrive swiftly and leave the same they do not concern themselves with human loss. It is already October and I have remarked to James that it were the exact same time when he first left us for the West. He says he is surprised to hear it that he did not remember at all. But I remember quite well he left for Truro and it were a sudden lonely time my brothers were older than I and labouring by then and I did not have much occasion to meet with my remaining classmates.

I think I envied him his going I were jealous that he would be seeing new parts of the country. I have never been to the places he speaks of now. Perhaps next year will bring me the opportunity.

We were walking to Forder for a service I were planned to take and to which he had offered to accompany me. I am not sure how much longer he is visiting and it occurred to me that he had come to say goodbye so I were pleased when we met and he did not raise the matter. We took the footpath along the river passing by the quay and talked to the workers there they were in good spirits. There were a beautiful sight as we stopped a train ran along further up by the bridge creating beautiful plumes of steam behind it rising in a line behind the trees. The clouds beyond it high and textured like sand after a tide furrowed in lines and mottled towards the hills.

Yet the beauty of that sight twisted somehow as it reached me and did not leave me feeling good. All I could consider were how often I had observed such scenes and how repetitive my path were. The same feeling as when you have been around a particular person for too long except in this case that person were the land my home. The familiarity I feel will kill me. I do not think I can stand it. I know I should leave this place.

I preached at Forder the lesson has already departed my mind. I do not have much trust in my own aspect presently so imagined myself to be other and occupied myself with the imitation of my betters. I preached as I thought my father or my Godfather might I trusted to their calm assurance the mantle of which I borrowed a while.

These chapels no longer feel like home I am uncomfortable in them and seem at every moment to have an itching to be away. There is something of me in these stones and wooden pews but they are heavy things to have and hard comfort that they offer. I would prefer the fields and the sky and the trees still standing. *I am the true vine* saith the Lord the living Word *he* does not shelter away among the stones and beams.

And after the service I were disappointed again felt neither *his* Grace nor *his* Glory it were as though I had partaken of something before I ate from *his* feast so that the taste of it were spoiled. I have never felt such despondency as I did in that church I do not know where such deep sadness in my former pleasures is come from. My soul settled in a depression and it seems recently as though it is often this way after I have been to worship.

I remember the Lord saying that some fell upon stony places *where they had not much earth* but I did not expect that plot to be in my own heart. O Lord show me the good ground the fertile places. Show me the earth where we can sow in expectation of an enduring harvest.

In the afternoon we attended a distress sale. James took me along to it and it were the first I have witnessed nor do I wish to see another. It is far from pleasing to see a person's things sold and to have no power over it I grew quite disturbed as we watched. Tables and chairs stacked upon each other waiting for the crowd to bid for them. A few meagre items of furniture a good oak dresser left on its side in the grass. James too were moved he were reluctant in saying that it were better to lose our earthly goods than lose our soul and he is right but we both knew that came as no consolation for the family who had lost them.

I remembered the abundance of produce we have seen at the chapel in the past week and I thought how this time were supposed to be a bounteous one for us a season when we improved our stocks to tide us over through the winter. Well it is clear that only those among us who have the means to do so will see much benefit and yet I feel there must be enough wealth among us to cater for the poorest if only it were shared. I were left to ponder the truth of *his* Word *The harvest is passed the summer is ended and we are not saved.*

And this is not the only reason my spirit is quite downcast I cannot avoid the truth of it. I am feeling deep sadness but I tell myself that it should not be indulged in it comes as a temptation tries to deceive our minds to question and doubt. For she has exchanged worlds for a better place and we have nothing to be sad for.

My journey home were refreshing it felt much needed. The beeches on the road to St Germans have turned at last to brilliant copper their leaves having nurtured for so long the colour of a thick purple dye. They shimmered in the wind a bright metallic aspect to them even in the gathering dark. The moon were new beautiful and white a thin curve like milk spilt around the edge of a cup. There is a clear sign of winter in the sky now the figure of Orion as he rises across the south falling nightly into the west. The skies are more familiar to me at this time of year the patterns form easily to my eyes perhaps it is the longer nights that I have had more opportunity to spend time beneath them. The huntsman seems an old friend returned after a summer away. Feels to be a good omen. It may be said that it is a pagan trait to examine the stars for portents still I think I have it right in my mind it is not the stars themselves that pattern knowledge for us except that they are an expression of the wonder of God who wrought them. After all did *he* not send a bright star to be a sign unto us? I do not believe I have it wrong. I greatly desire to find hope in these things.

30

Another night is gone following on swiftly from the last and there were sickness in my chest today when I awoke. I felt the earth to be slipping away. Felt the tide of time to have turned again pulling a little more from me. The far depths beckoning.

I put my breakfast aside I could not stomach it. I think the dampness of the air in this room does me no good I would soon exchange it for another.

In his last years back when I were still a boy my father suffered near constant pain. Shards of iron that might have been forged hot on the fire formed in his kidneys and he were unable to pass water without crying out in desperation a sound he tried to muffle and keep within himself and which emerged as a fearful low groan pulled from his innards. When I were very young I would run from the sound and hide in the furthest corner of the farm trying to rid myself of the chill it shook me with. I grew old in a house of suffering and no one can tell me what I have endured.

And it is true that I were much sobered by seeing my father's suffering. Though another truth is that it were a strange thing to see him in that anguished state because I did not know what he felt I were too young to imagine it too young to comprehend anything of what it truly were to suffer. I lived alongside him and he suffered and I did not and among the feelings that were aroused in me some were shameful indeed. The relief I felt that *it were not me*. Now I have finally learned this small piece of wisdom that unless we have experienced it ourselves we cannot know what it is our imaginations fail us we are too caught up in our own condition. How little feeling we have for our fellow man that we can forget their pains so easily ignore their troubles even though they be our own blood we must be taught to keep the thought of others close in mind.

Well I too am tired from labouring in the vineyard of the Lord I have yet to see the reward. I have never felt my body to be so heavy as now so much of a weight which requires dragging with me. Something I need *transport*. At the forge I am always stopping to rest my arms can hardly hold the tools.

I think of the chapels I have visited which in their emptiness remind me of hollow shells that crack open and reveal that the sought-for kernel has withered away.

At night I dream of wide spaces with a broad roof above extending to the horizons an oppressive mass as though it would fall on me and just myself beneath it the whole span coming down on the single point where I am curled in terror. They come as nightmares those dreams and I awake clammy with sweat trying to swallow the horror. Even in open spaces there is something hemming me in the fields are oppressive the sky presses low.

From these troublesome thoughts the sickness has finally emerged and two days have been lost to a fever. The fever is fear it makes me sick to my bones it affects my brain. I cannot feel even grief it dulls my most powerful emotions. It turns my stomach and twice this week has dislodged my breakfast. Tuesday I lost my food by the stream on my way to work I were terrible sick. Then it persisted the next day and I could think of nothing other than how wretched I were. My body seems like a weak thing I thought there were iron in it but no it is only flesh and frail too frail. I cannot abide it. I cannot abide to feel it in me I am a worthless and unhealthy thing.

Harr found something in her sickness which brought her close to our Master. But it is hard to see. I do not understand how that were for her. My struggles are nothing compared to hers they do not seem so profound neither do I attain grace

136

through them. It is as though there is something attached to this particular sickness which is *doubt* and prevents me from summoning up the joy required for adversity. I have believed that sickness can be good for us well I do not feel much improved by it. Merely shorn of my illusions that this world is anything other than a trial that the path is narrow and the sufferings that beset man on the path are many.

I am reminded strongly of the sickness I endured as a boy. But to be ill as a child is a different matter you have your parents to nurse you and give you the confidence that you will soon be whole again. Your father's hand hard on your forehead. You do not have to face alone the falling fear. Well I have no one now to give me that confidence no one who can be entrusted with the matter of restoring me to health. We become children again when we are sick hoping that someone will take care of us and there is only God if *he* comes in *his* mercy. So my mind is chewed with worry I am left to wonder how I can be a force in my life if I am vulnerable and weak unfit to rise from my bed. Even the simple things are beyond me. If I remain sick and unable to work I am become just as my father were yet with no family of my own to support me. I am not so much younger now than he were when he sickened.

Even the days I have been able to work have produced little for I can hardly keep my mind on what I do. My concentration is broken. There is only the pain itself and sickness in the centre it is hard enough even to rest or pray for the strength I so sorely lack.

How will I live if I cannot afford to?

What recourse do I have?

It causes me to think of dying and I have found some pleasure in imagining the glory of passing in Christ and at last exchanging worlds it would be a blessed relief. I have loved this world enough but there is no Heaven in it now that I can see. And perhaps it were a better thing to die than suffer alone and in fear. But then I am filled with remorse because that relief I imagined were for escaping the sufferings of this life and not in welcoming the one to come.

I must trust that God will provide. I have read my Bible and searched for *his* promises to us and found these words from Exodus 16th Chapter: *And when the dew had gone up there was on the face of the wilderness a fine flake-like thing fine as hoarfrost on the ground.* They seemed full of promise once these words but now the sentence appeared strange to my eyes blurring in front of me as though it were written in a language I did not know just a pretty script bereft of meaning.

31

A Sabbath and I were finally well enough to attend school in the morning I felt grieved to see the sad state of it only four students there and William not among them the superintendent himself a half hour late. Then chapel later in the morning but with it came depression and I did not feel an urge to continue that way for the remainder of the day.

So I have left the tracts aside. I have let be the sermons that are already there. If they have been read already they will stand for another month or so and will suffer being read again. And if they are unread then they will remain unread still.

Though I have not fully shaken my weariness I have been out to walk. I went to feel closer to God. Walked up on the hills desirous to see the land opening out about me and restoring the elements in our lives to their proper place. My legs were very painful but I ignored it as much as I could lengthened my stride into a march to work the stiffness off.

It has been a blustery day. Felt to me that there were something in the wind like the promise of rain. Tiny movements occupied the space in front of my eyes something in the air darting around strange flecks of dark so that I wondered if some spirit were crowding me. The wind were strong the leaves on the ground already wet with decay. Making a sodden swirl when the gusts took them up. The trees have changed to their autumn aspects now are half-fallen into winter loss. The fields are emptied of their crops are just earth dusted with dry colour appearing yellow in the sun.

And I feel I am come into a foreign land. The *shape* of it has not altered but still I do not know it. Something of the essence of the land has changed the trees are not as they were. They seem to mock the past are become grotesque impostors of truth. Half the beauty of the world is gone from it. I trust it is a dysfunction in me that it will not last but I think I know now how it felt to be cast out of Eden into a barren world.

I know the land now. I have been out and looked on it and it is not what I thought it were let me say what the land is like.

> *It is a land of hidden things its horizons are near.*
> *It is not as it once were.*
> *The land is alive but that life is sickening and ugly and*
> *sucking on us and God is not in it.*
> *The land has no centre only dirt. There is black under*
> *the green the trees are hollow beneath their bark.*
> *The land is full of fears as though it had adopted our*
> *own it is drenched in them more thoroughly than*
> *the rain.*

I think I do not know much of fear. I have had no reason to be afraid. Perhaps once in my childhood when I became lost in the valley up from St Eve and thought I knew my way but the path I followed did not bring me home it kept me in the woods they seemed to continue without end and I could not find my bearings. I were afraid to run ahead in case I were taking myself further away from home.

I wandered crying that day without making progress in any direction and I were lucky in the end to find a woman coming the other way who took my hand and brought me back. My father had no sympathy he did not understand how I could lose myself so close to home. For years afterwards it brought a sickly feeling to me when I thought of it I felt dizzy with shame. I want to rid myself of these things they should not trouble us still.

Dusk had come on my walk and the pain in my legs worsened again I were half glad of it for it offered some occupation to my mind. But then I thought of Harr and as I did so some nausea returned swelled in me like grain sitting in water a far worse thing to suffer and I could not escape it no matter how hard I walked. There is naught so powerful as sickness. Nausea corrupts the spirit afflicts its victims with fear and doubt. The whole world appears infected when I look at it. The green of the trees and the brown of the earth are swooning colours. Everything originating from my belly and returning to the same. When we speak of what is at the core of us we say our *hearts* well I think our *bellies* represent the essence of it equally.

The sky dropped close and brought rain. It came like a strange dream to the land left it an unsettled place and grey too. I did not feel I had the energy for it so I came home.

It were cold in the kitchen and shivering I took the bellows and tried to find some life in the stove but nothing showed. So I rebuilt the wood and lit it waiting for the warmth which were slow to come. Then put some milk on to boil with a little salt and flour. In my tiredness I closed my eyes and dwelt on the day my thoughts running together aiming towards sleep caught myself just in time to stop the broth before it boiled over. It scalded my mouth as I drank it felt good the only warm thing in me. But it awoke my longing for home too the milk here is thinner than what we have on the farm the taste of it not much richer than water of course my landlady would not use the best of it on me. It is another angering thought because I have paid for what I have here and she shears off what I am owed sooner than her hands fall to idleness.

The next morning sickness woke me pulling me into unpleasant consciousness the shock of it enough to make me curse. My belly churning I retched bile into my throat as I sat up then vomited on the stone floor beside my bed. When I tried to move my legs protested I were in agony and my back too the pain seeming to progress like an infection from one part of my body to the next.

I lay there for a full day and no one came. The smell of my evacuation ugly almost enough to make me vomit more. It drives me into myself this sickness but everyone seems blind to it. No one came from the forge to see why I had not come to work and I heard my landlady in her kitchen and knew she would have seen that I had not left the house but she bustled on with her chores and did not once knock on my door. So I were angry at her and would not crawl across the room to call for her.

I am tired of the sickness recurring it feels like I have had more than my portion of this one. I feel like an old man suffering the weariness of age which came too quickly upon me. There is a dark truth in my heart I have come to understand that I cannot live this way. I would sooner die than continue such suffering please God may it be taken from me. How desperate it seems. How impossible that man can endure such things. I have said before that I do not know much of fear but it seems to me that sickness and fear afflict me both in a similar way I think they are made of the same stuff and there is no doctor that can cure them.

I have come into dark spaces. There were better days I know but the happiness I felt then is not in my heart now. When I were young I knew neither death nor suffering and it were a better thing to live that way.

32

The fever returned that night and for two days after I starved myself until it burned away. Sweated it from me believing it were of the kind of which it is said it comes forth by nothing but prayer and fasting. My landlady were alarmed at my inclination to fast she is hardly the type to understand that self-deprivation might bring us closer to our Master. She brought me bread but I would not spoil my lips with it not until I felt it had gone from me and the bread were dry and hardening.

Well I have been left feeling weak and light-headed but somehow cleaner as though I had been properly washed by my own sweat. I think the heat of the fever works as does a crucible for metal all the impurities float from it. And I feel new-born too my legs shaking and unable to bear my weight like those of a foal come feeble and guiltless into the world.

James came to visit and seeing me in a weak and reduced state he fetched some soup and sat with me while I ate it. I were so tired afterwards that I cried could just curl up and weep exhaustion. James reached over me placed his hand on my shoulder and kept it there a long time until I felt recovered. His eyes closed in prayer as he did so.

I am sorry I said. I must seem like a child.

It is no trouble.

I tried to order my thoughts and words to find the things I wanted to ask him it were not easy. His lips moved he finished his prayers.

Do you not think we could see things better then?

As children you mean? I am sure there's much which seems simpler to them.

That is not what I meant I said. I think truthfully we were closer to some things and knew them better then we grow old and get more distant from them. I cannot explain too well.

Perhaps you are right he said and I thought he were being polite in saying this I were not sure he had understood.

I have something to ask you I said.

It had been fretting inside of me the last few days. A memory that had recurred now that I were sick and I wished to see if he shared.

Do you remember an adventure we had one summer? We were ten or thereabouts. We ran away for the night to stay in the woods.

He thought a moment.

A little I think he said.

Ah I said. I were disappointed the memory were not so fresh to him.

Why do you ask? he said.

No reason I thought to say *No reason other than it is drenched in longing as I think of it. No reason except that it surges in me now and speaks of everything that has been unfulfilled.* We had met near his house at Newbridge by the mill where the path runs round the pool where he were sent for his baths. We followed the waterway up from it. The mill stream is diverted from the Lynher a clear river with rocky bed overhung with long-necked trees. An ancient wood mossed over in its darkest places. Shadow-streaked glades that excited our imaginations almost with a fever. And in thickening trees far up along the cool cut of the stream the remains of a small dwelling. The roof complete but swaybacked with tiles a few of them missing. Doors and windows just toothless maws in the ivy-covered stone. An abandoned place in the woods we had heard of we had been told it belonged to a woodcutter that he had died out there and because the place were now lost that he lay there still. Well we spent the night there and there were no body nor much sign that the place ever had been owned so perhaps that part of it were just a story. I doubt we slept much

144

half through fear of the encircling woods and half through talking. I remember imagining that we might own that place and live there. If the world ran the way that children think it does. Or if time had ceased then. But it did not and the next morning the pull to stay were lessened and we knew we must leave.

I have not thought of that night for a long time though the beating I received when I returned home were one that ought to resound in my mind still so painful were it. Seems that memories endure when it appears that they have been long forgotten.

And I do not know why it comes to me now. Perhaps it is simply that that time were the last of it. The last moments I had when I were a child and still free. I could not explain it to my friend now.

It is the only time I have left home I said. I remembered how much fun it were. And beautiful. Nothing more.

He looked at me with a curious eye.

The West is beautiful too he said. You would like it. The cliffs make excellent walking.

It seemed he did not have much regard for the past that he were happily rooted in our present hour without feeling it being lost to him. But I were pleased he had come to talk of the West the thought of it has been preying on my mind.

I cannot come I said. It would be foolish to leave my apprenticeship now I have worked hard for what I have and could hardly find something new.

There are smithies in the West too he said. I am sure someone would take you on. If you came in the right season you could labour until then.

I hardly see my family as it is. I cannot come.

But I muttered the words and were drifting into a reverie as I spoke my thoughts tiredly moving on to the next thing. I do not know how much time passed. I closed my eyes the lids sticky with the residue of tears. It felt like I were not done with that there were fresh water still waiting to well up.

145

There is something upsetting you still he said.

Oh I said it is nothing.

There were something in your mind made you frown.

Well. Perhaps. I were thinking of an invalid I used to visit. She has passed away and I quite miss visiting her.

The blind girl? he said. You told me about her. Are you surprised to hear it? You often talked about the strength of her faith. I didn't know she had died. I'm sorry. Do you doubt she is with our Lord now? You should rejoice at that.

But I feel the pain of her loss I said. I should not be made to feel this way when she has gone to happiness.

Then grieve he said. It is natural.

It is grief. He were right about that. I think she opened in me some sense of the Lord some capacity for love that cannot now be fulfilled. That there is nothing else to equal it and everything must seem inferior. But not even grief would come only sickness.

She were beautiful in suffering I said. So frail.

And I were appalled by what I had said.

You were in love with her?

I were unprepared for the question. It seemed an intimate thing to ask I am not much given to discussing my feelings on such matters. Well we were friends I did not mind it.

I loved her in Christ I said and there were truth in it.

I am sorry he said and it were no apology merely sympathy heart-felt and quite simply stated.

It is just . . . just that I cannot escape thinking on it. That perhaps it were a punishment for me. Because I had done some wrong.

Why would you be punished? he said. Why is it a judgement on you? You know it cannot be. You should not think that way.

He looked at me with something I felt to be pity in his eyes as though he saw my understanding to be fettered and I felt a surge of anger at him in my weakness though it passed quickly away.

I don't know I said. I am sorry. I did not mean to bother you with it.

My thoughts churned in my brain it felt as though I did not own them.

Charles? he said.

Yes.

I am leaving soon. Returning home.

A shame I said I felt it deeply.

I do not like to leave you this way he said. When you are well again you should leave here. Come with me. It does you no good to stay.

And I were glad he had asked me directly I had wished for it and as he said it a vision of the West rose to my mind like pumping blood sudden and dizzying then fading back. It took a moment before the weakness swept past me.

I am only here a little while longer he were saying. There is nothing more I can do for my family except stay these few days. I must be with them now. But I will come and visit before I leave.

I half listened to him my mind were elsewhere. Seemed that it were buzzing with thoughts and words forced upon it.

Why are you here? I asked.

What do you mean? he said he were quite surprised.

I do not know you. I should be alone in this.

You know me he said. Of course you know me. You're not well. You aren't making much sense now.

Well it is clear to me I said.

I am sorry then he said. I don't understand.

What do you want here James? I asked I do not know why I said it. You do not belong here. You have left and things have changed which you do not see. You should not have come back. The place is different now. You cannot understand.

He watched me without speaking. He met my eye I buried my head I could not look at him. When he spoke his voice were gentle felt like I were being lowered back onto soft blankets.

I have to go he said. I am sorry. You have been unwell. Illness makes us feel strange things sometimes. You should sleep. You will feel better tomorrow.

I did not even know what I were saying. It felt as though we had already parted that day and I do not remember the fact of his leaving. I stayed home yet it seemed somehow as though I were the one who left that I had taken the wide path the easy way and that I had gone alone.

Where does our bravery come from? *Lift up thine eyes unto the hills* we are told but the hills are old and speak of other things.

33

It is November. A fine day late in the season. The first day for some time I have been up from my bed. We have had unusual warmth in the afternoon. In the shortening days the touch of sunlight is restorative and I have raised my face unto it as though it were the pure unfolding glory of the Lord.

But I do not feel it does me much good. The darkness in my heart is a disc that matches the size of the sun seems to obscure the bright light. It came to me as a friend the darkness to embrace me. Stood by my side and rested an arm across my shoulders as though it knew me. Then turned me towards it and pulled me close and it entered my heart and prayer has not loosened its hold. And it is heavy and set in me so perhaps it will come to fill me the way my faith has done.

34

The next day were a Thursday and our class meeting were due in the evening but I returned early from God's house because I were alone there. I took some time to read from a book which had been recommended me by a parishioner the account of two children who had much faith in the Lord. They were taken away from the evils of this world at the early ages of nine and eleven years and it were pleasing to read their story I found great reassurance with their simplicity and trust in Christ as their Saviour.

Well those children are gone unto *him* now and are reaping their reward no doubt I trust that I will be encouraged by their example.

I think on all I have left undone.

My health seems somewhat recovered but I have slept uneasily the last nights though I worked hard to push myself into weariness. In the mornings I sit exhausted watching the dust that fills the kitchen become living sparks in sunlight's forge. I have stayed there a long while until my imagination had convinced me that the dust had come to life. Tiny insects born of light alone. In the past I have taken this apparition for a reminder of the Holy Spirit among us that *he* is all around us even in the smallest of things.

It has been hard to rouse myself and awake to the life of the day minor distractions come into my mind and I have lain in bed until late and thought on them and lost much time this way.

I feel afflicted with trouble. The days that come are beyond the reach of my arms and offer nothing save an encumbered future while the days already at my shoulder are too quickly past and we shall have no more of them. Perhaps I am still sick perhaps afraid something coils in me and gnaws at the muscles and nerves. If the enemy revealed itself to me he would be easier to fight I could put some hold on him. If he came as a demon in the night a vast face in the air a great wind blowing. But *he* says that the battle we fight is not of flesh and blood and my earthly strength counts for naught.

Great acts of healing are not so far gone into the past when my Master reached down with *his* hand and touched earthly flesh and filled it with white fire and made that flesh whole again its afflictions stripped away. I long to see such wonders again. Heaven and earth were close then but this black land seems far away from Paradise so it seems the two are growing apart.

Twenty eight years will soon be past for me. So much of my allotted portion on this earth. Well I feel how quick the days go but still I will not seize them. It seems as though I have willed the last year gone from me that I did not awaken to it until it were already past and lost from my life.

35

Still I have been to work and struggled on with the days. I have lost my opportunity to return home Mr Coad has not been pleased that I have had so many days away from the forge and I will not see a free day again until Christmas. My mother will be sad.

Friday on my way back to Quethiock I found time to attend a temperance meeting held in the parish church by Tideford. It is a large church there the front of it very impressive indeed with a great central window split into three lancet panes with intricate ironwork surrounding. I wish I understood a little more of its history. If it were built by men whose names are common still whose families endure here. Such times I come to regret the simple building styles of our own chapels though of course there is merit in simplicity too and much to be said for filling the rooms with men rather than riches. Inside the church are many rows of varnished pews though the wood mostly unworn. Enough room for three hundred I should think a much larger space than I am used to. Sun lights hang on thick chains from the ceiling it becomes a bright gathering place when they are lit.

There were representatives of four churches there. A few members of the parish church had come as well as some from the Wesleyan community and the Quakers. Then one woman I recognized as a Catholic had joined with us for the meeting I were not sure what to make of it. Of course it is pleasing that she has attached herself to this crusade of ours and found in her heart an evangelism for abstinence but I do not know what to feel about our congregations mingling so easily. There is bad history between us and many evil acts done I trust this brief union shall be a peaceful one that we may keep the proper enemy in our sight.

We had an earnest speaker he were a just man and a preacher of the truth. He provided us his testimony I were sad Mr Pendray were not there to hear it I think their stories had much in common. But the man spoke at too great a length outlining the sin across the country and it were a depressing landscape he painted for us. He described the geography of our parish compared the ale flowing through it to our God-provided rivers the Tiddy and the Lynher and said we must choose from which source our refreshment came. He said the working man were worst affected by it that they were the trees planted and their roots had given up on water and were soaked now with drink which would poison them all the corruption spreading further from there. And he continued in this way for a long time well it were an interesting approach I have not heard before but a bleak one too and I wish he had spoken more of his own redemption.

My spirit is presently too sensitive to the mood of such matters and I were despondent after the meeting I did not gather with the others I could not bear their company. I feel as though I am losing everything I yearned to have in my life and everything I desired to be. Christian fellowship is a precious thing to be guarded with great care and somehow I have forfeited the reward of it I have left open the doors.

My legs felt stronger last night and I have had an urge to test them I rose this morning a little before five and took a walk on the hill the dawn were a beautiful one when it came and the scenery grand my thoughts were carried beyond this world. I saw the hills adorned with thick grass. My feet grew wet and my legs felt very weak but it were worth it to see the sparkling dew. The trees now are stripped thin mostly denuded of leaves but finally appearing restored to their proper nature and everything again almost as it were before. I wonder if I will have the same feeling for it. The land still has its shadows about it but it seems to have that divine life

inhabiting it afresh and I recognized enough of its old character to enjoy the walk.

I trod over the top of the hills on drying heath the twigs
crackling under my step. Came down through cool covered
groves and into a meadow which were thick with grass and
colours the green transforming into yellows and browns.
There were a kestrel hovering above it appeared as though it
had been pinned to the sky and were flapping in an effort to
free itself. In the air an unusual freshness a pleasurable
autumn scent I took great gulps of it to replenish what I had
lost in the sickness.

And I thought how strange it were that some days forgiveness seemed to come so easily.

A short way to the east I came by Blunts a small hamlet the
cottages there looked very nice in the day and I felt revived
by the sight. But when I came to pass them I saw that two of
the homes were empty and their stones cold I knew they had
belonged to miners who lost their jobs and are gone for
America or Australia and the new mines they dig there. I
wished better fortunes for them but it were a sad sight to see
their homes abandoned. They turn over their histories not for
great wealth but merely for hope the promise of new seams
attracting them as though they were iron to its lodestone.

Things have been well here while we have had the mines.
There has been work for families and we have depended
upon them. But they will hollow out the earth until there is no
more profit from it and what then. The whole land will be
empty the old mines in the West are nearly done with they
have reached as deep as they can they have uncovered the tin
beneath the copper and dug that too. And it seems they have
mined from the spirit to a similar extent they have exhausted
the life in it so the chapels are also empty.

I have been thinking what it might be to leave this place to
follow the flow of men away from here. If I finish my apprenticeship it would not be hard. I could leave for the West
where the churches still have their ground or take a boat to

Australia I have seen enticements of free passage for skilled labour the same as one brother of mine were lured by in years past. I could finish my apprenticeship and remove my skills for a distant land. I wonder how God's work is done there. I cannot imagine how it would be I do not know if I have the courage.

Such were the thoughts that occupied me during the day but that is all they remained just a tumble of ideas half-images of life and nothing coming that seemed as if I could plan it.

Well I had not gone on my walk entirely without purpose I went to find James and spend some time with him before he leaves us. I have felt a need to talk with him since he came by when I were sick and I said things I did not understand for some reason I were angry at him. Even though it were he who had been kind to me and come to find me when I were suffering alone and needed to be found. So when I reached as far as the Lynher I turned north towards Newbridge following the river up and it were not so late in the afternoon when I reached the mill.

There were no answer though at his family's house I had hoped that his sister at least might be home. If she were still sick she should not be about much I took her absence for a good sign that she had recovered. I looked around to see if anyone were there but Newbridge were quiet. I waited a long while but grew restless in the end it did not appear as though anyone were coming. It seemed a great shame. I did not think I would have the opportunity to return my duties at work would keep me.

I were very tired but there are so few hours of light available now so I stayed out longer than I should have walking the hills until dusk came and the night followed. And it were worth it for I were afforded a glorious sight of Heaven. No moon just the sky bright with stars strewn like grit from the Hand of God. They seemed to appear swiftly and took my breath away with their number. I could not take my eyes from the sight were forgetful of the path and kept tripping over its edge. A searing bright girdle across the height of the sky and almost every bit of the night filled with them. I have heard it said that there are stars enough in number one for each and every person in the world and tonight I could believe that it were true.

So it were a good day spent beneath the sun and then the stars and for a while I found a little peace.

Found myself shaking and hungry when I came home. I sat and ate all my energy focussed on the eating quite forgetting my surrounds. Only when I had finished did it occur to me that I had spent the whole day alone and would have been happier for some company like that day earlier in the year I had spent with James. My old friends are close to leaving once again it may be this way for a long time.

I felt I were going to bed quietly I did not wish to awaken my landlady but she must have been sitting by her door listening out for me she emerged quickly as I went past to my room. She had hostility stored in her expression it seemed she had been saving it for me and could not let the chance pass to expend it. She held a sheet of paper in her hands she flicked it at my face in annoyance nearly catching my eye. The whole intent of her anger finding expression in her body and leaning her forward with it. Reminded me of a weasel for she is quite a small thing but streaked with viciousness.

It is not right to have visitors without arrangement and then not even be here for them she said.

Who came then? I asked.

He spent half the day here and I felt obliged to offer him some tea. It is right unreasonable. I should charge you for it.

For tea? I do not even know who came I said. And I were not expecting anyone you were not obliged to do anything.

Don't you tell me what I have been obliged to do. You are in no position for that and standing in my own house too.

She near spat at me as she said it. So clearly she were not ready to retreat on the matter and I needed to listen for long minutes to the elaboration of her complaints until I got from her the information that it were *that youth* James who had come. At the same time I had gone along to see him he had been likewise compelled. He had waited much of the day and then borrowed some paper and left me a letter I took it from her I went into my room. I am sure she read it while she had it I do not care.

Brother Wenmoth,

Having hoped to see you again I regret the need of leaving this letter for you to find – I trust you have been well & involving yourself today in good work – But my new home is calling me & I have a train to Penzance this evening. I am sorry to have missed you – I have wanted to tell you how good it has been to have seen you after many years when we did not have the opportunity. & how good too to be reminded of our youth – You have refreshed my memory of many things I had forgotten & my heart is richer for it. Although we have had reason to mourn lately I shall return to work with a glad spirit.

I trust your absence today is a good sign of your health – I have been unhappy to think of you suffering & I know it has brought you to doubting but I have great confidence that the path you walk is the Lord's & that His light be but briefly hidden from you. I have prayed for your swift recovery & will continue to do so. For though we have never been far removed from illness & death it has not ceased to be a mystery to us & God withholds the last of the knowledge of this world. & the remainder is left to our faith – A most powerful device – A small portion of it shall be sufficient for us all.

You should not be afraid to persevere & you will soon find that He has guided your feet through. Do not doubt that there is purpose in it – How glorious that our every breath is overseen by Him! So let us not be dismayed by the struggles of this life but rest in peace for the promise of Glory we have been given – God having provided something better for us.

*My father & mother send you their best wishes & you should
know you are welcome to visit them they would receive you
gladly. Similarly I will always be happy for word of your mother
& brothers – I trust that they are secure in the hands of the Lord
& that you will relay my greetings to them when you are next
home.*

*I invest in this letter an invitation to visit us in the West
when you are fully well. I trust to see you soon & in good health
– We shall look forward to hearing of your arrival. There are
many hills waiting for our steps on them & good climbs on
which to test our stamina.*

*Until then go in God & may the peace of the Lord go with
you. I think in the Lord's eyes we remain the children we once
were. We will see us soon.*

*Your brother in Christ our Saviour
James*

And it were a kind letter a good thing to receive but it seemed
somehow foreign in nature as though I felt the kindness to me
were misplaced. That he spoke of things in me which were
not there.

Since I read it I have dwelt on some of his words he said
that *we remain the children we once were* so in the evening when
I had time I read the Bible and went to look within myself for
signs of that child but I needed to look deep. The weight of
duty has worn on me and there were not much of that old
feeling remaining so perhaps it is long gone and already lost.

36

James has left us then I suppose it were expected. And Harr is gone several weeks already I wonder if even she had a good death if in her final sufferings she did not feel some spark of fear. Though I am sure Dr Coryton provided me with a reliable account the truth is that I do not know what were in her heart at the end. Those we have loved were always inaccessible to us no better than shades beside us. And what if her illness were not after all from God but something that would give her up to death would turn over her blessed spirit and though her faith were strong it would linger until that faith were spent and then at that moment take her. It is an unpleasant thought it came to me idly and has bothered me since I cannot get comfortable for thinking of it.

My thoughts of late cause me much unhappiness they seem of a darker bent than is usual but I have found nothing to lift them. I find myself when I have time reading again and again from the Beatitudes hoping their beauty will instil itself in my heart and allay the noisome and persistent pain.

This evening I were called to see Mrs Truscott she has grown very old and she cannot get the confidence in Christ that she wants. It is hard to remain faithful to the end. What comfort I could provide her I did not know I think there were none I had for her. Just platitudes the same words we use to console others when we ourselves do not know their fear.

She were sat wrapped in a shawl it looked woollen though old and the holes in it widened with time and pulling. It could not have afforded much warmth. Her hands were curled with age too twisted for darning I wondered if I might ask someone in the village to mend it for her. But who would I ask whose charity has not deserted them.

The sky at sunset an apocalyptic red it reminded me that each day might be the last. We have only one life and it is too short. We have no opportunity to mend our mistakes. Those we have lost will remain lost they will not be returned to us. All my childhood friends that I see no longer well I long for their company again for our old sports and games but they will not revisit. We came alone into the world and that is how it shall be at the end for us on our deathbeds going solitary into the darkness to see what more awaits us. Taking with us nothing that we have won here.

And I have kept up my visits the remainder of the week I went one more time to visit Harr's mother though it were a hard walk to make when I thought of how pleasurable it has been in the past. It were an easy way once would fall behind me quickly when I could dwell on the sweet promise of time spent with her.

That were Monday evening and so washday in the village the almshouses had become a masted ship raised with the sails of drying sheets. But by Mrs French's house there were nothing no sign of her activity that day and I were surprised when the door opened to my tentative knock. She paused when she saw me I thought I were unexpected but she invited me in. The house seemed entirely empty. I thought at first she must have been required to sell some of their possessions but then I realized more likely that it were people the house missed. I asked for William but she said that he were labouring now. I were sad to hear that. William is just a boy and I imagined she meant he had gone to work at the quay. I wished I had some money to give to them it seemed that they were in grievous need of it.

I felt then that she were not so pleased to see me after all but I thought that if that were so she would not have invited me in I did not know what I might have done to disappoint her.

We sat in the kitchen for a while she is a woman hard pressed by grief and having lost so much in her life yet she bears it in silence.

She has grown old again since I visited the last of her dark hair is finally become white. She wore the same paramatta she wore after her husband's death it is old and worn the black fading into grey at the seams. She tires more easily now. Her glance is a breaking bottle which collapses into liquid. I were ashamed to realize that I had visited her only once since Harr has gone in her grief she too needs my time she has little remaining family for consolation. But I do not feel the Lord in me to offer her comfort only the memory of what I might have said in the past and it comes so weak from my tongue it barely suffices to convince even me.

So I did not stay long. I did not want to ask how she were coping now I were too afraid of the answer. And it seemed we could find nothing else to speak of.

As I were thinking of leaving we were interrupted by a man come down from the estate and I were glad that someone had come to break into our silence. He were bringing her a fish to cook a gift from the estate so I were cheered to see that there were someone else who remembered her and had her interests in mind. But she seemed in two minds whether to cook it now or wait for William and I felt I were somehow in the way. I would have liked to see William and to have had the chance to give him some reassurance but it seemed that this were not the time so I left the poor woman be.

It is cruel for the young to be taken before they had their time for parents to be orphaned of their children. And I am reminded that Harr went alone without her family and I trust my Master walked with her that her father might have been there before her and that she herself will wait for those she has loved.

Well it were a painful visit. I do not have much of Harr left to comfort myself with. The few remaining memories I own are quite precise the bulk of our time has been lost.

One afternoon I sat there in the warm room and a narrow beam of sun came angled in through the small window. As the hours passed the beam burned slowly across the room moving up the foot of the bed and along the sheet. Harr drifted into sleep her face peaceful with rest. Tiny spasms flickered through her body as she fell into dreams so that it appeared she must be woken but she were insensible to them. It were a wonderful thing to behold appeared as though her body were brushed by some other hand and I remember feeling sure then that this sickness were from the Lord that *he* had taken her soul as she offered it to *him*.

And the time I called by to find her sitting with William when he took out an old slate he used for writing and handed it to her. Her fingers closed around the short chalk holding it between her thumb and three fingers bunched together. She touched the tip of the chalk to the slate and pushed her arm to move so that the memory of how she used to write would tug at her hand and form the script by instinct. In near perfect handwriting she wrote out her name three times. The lines sloping a little but the letters smoothly formed. I were forced to think that there is so much the body knows that does not require our mind nor eyes to guide it.

Harriet French
Harriet French
Harriet French

she wrote and asked how it looked. William told her that the writing were neater than his own then he took the board and wiped it blank as though to hide it from her what she had done.

On some later visit I asked if I could fetch a slate for her so that she could write again.

Oh no she said to me. It would be a silly thing. What use do I have for it now?

And she seemed quite happy though I felt there were no reason she should not write for she could do it so well and who would expect that?

And once more near the last time I were able to visit nothing remains but a singular memory like a simple picture painted in my mind that I can call to view. It is the end of my visit. She makes a slight turn of her head in my direction as I leave. Her eyes are bright with colour I cannot believe they do not see me. She is smiling to bid me goodbye there is no pain in the look only satisfaction and I believe I shared for one moment that rapture she knows the true happiness of her soul. I have never given much thought to the question of her physical beauty but when this memory comes to my mind as it does often now I am given to thinking that she were very beautiful indeed and I am sad that I will not look on her face again.

These memories will not last. Already the details of her face seem muddied the precise lines of her expression falling from my mind like flowers once bloomed and dying another reminder of our mortality. I do not wish to outlive these things. I do not wish to live without them. And I am angry at it angry at what goes on inside of me that I have no control over and I am boiled to heat and simmering tears but I can do nothing about it.

If I could have my time. If I could have my time again and live those days over. Then nothing of this. I would have allowed nothing of it to pass neither one hour nor one minute. If I had known the time were so soon fled I would have had more of it I would have taken more.

I feel it has been stolen from me and it seems like a terrible injustice. So little has been given me to own so few things of any value and yet all I cared for has been ruined like a crop lost to pestilence. I have come to feel a great greed inside of me a hunger for those hours gone an insidious appetite that tells me there is something of the Devil about this desire. *Eternal life* awaits if I am worthy of that glory but it seems as though it is life already gone I have more craving for.

This soreness will not be lifted there is no recourse on earth. I have seen it in my dreams the past memories of happier times and I know my arms twitch and reach out to gather those scenes to me but they encounter nothing. I awake to emptiness and my small room seems terrifyingly vast around me. The grief I experience is a shuddering in my belly the feel of a ship grounding in shallow waters so how should I battle against it? If I could I would grasp hold of the things I once had I would fight with full force and have my Heaven. But it is past. All past. The time is gone and will not be returned to me.

And I have never had such longing for anything in my life not even for my own soul to be saved. So why does it come so powerful now and only for those things I have no authority over for things I cannot have?

37

Three days ago in the evening a beggar came to our door and I listened from my room as my landlady refused him alms and sent him away told him to go the Church if he wanted for anything. As though the Church were something apart from her. Well she does not have much it is true but he had far less than us I expect only a barn to sleep in and she would not even go to the kitchen to fetch him some food. No doubt she feared he would steal something from the house when she turned her back. It is quite a contrast with the portrait she paints of herself when she talks. Her self-image as a generous woman. She is always telling me how kind she is to have taken me in how well she treats me as though I had no mother of my own and did not pay her for everything I receive here. I think she has never had charity inculcated in her heart certainly she has none of it to spare.

I went out and hurried after the poor man gave him a six-pence I felt obliged to though I could scarce afford it. I have been counting my money carefully and am hard pressed.

And my disappointment in her has endured. Today when we both had a few minutes of peace which coincided I were disinclined to sit with her but could not find an excuse to refuse some tea. Well normally I do not listen to her so much but she were talking of Australia and lately I have found the subject to be of great interest. Evidently Richard has written her a letter suggesting she take the boat to Australia and live with his family there.

But she says to me: I do not know how he can ask. And: How does he think he can ask me to leave?

Though in all honesty I am not sure what she has to keep her company here except a hard-defended loneliness. Oh I understand the desire to stay I would greatly miss these hills if I chose to leave. And she has this house. But she could let it go it is only stones and she has nothing else to lose other than her life inside its walls. There are plenty enough who have chosen to go so why should not she?

Where would you live if I left? she asked me. As though she had ever worried about my home.

I asked her many questions about Australia and what Richard has said of it in his letters I were curious to know what he wrote about the opportunities for improvement there. But clearly she did not care about such things her mind were more occupied by the wrench of moving and the enormity of the passage.

It is such a long journey she said. The discomfort and indignity of it. I am not used to transport. He cannot ask me.

The ships are sturdier now I said. They are used to the voyages I think it is not so hazardous as it were.

But she were quite upset by it. It seems she has a terror of boats. I wonder if she has ever seen the ocean.

Still you should consider it I said. Once the trip were over your son would be there for you.

Her face crinkled with distaste she did not like to hear from me what she should do. There were a sharp retort on her tongue but it did not find its way her face broke into sadness she began to weep before me. Leaned forward and dropped her face into her hands. Ran tears between her fingers. I were moved to comfort her but it did not seem right to touch her. We had no relationship that would allow it.

I cannot go she said her voice were strained and contorted by sobbing. It's too late for it now. I am too old. It is too much change to expect of me I cannot go now. I have things hard enough here he cannot expect me to pick up and go as though I were still a young woman. And what life would he offer me there? I'm too old to work again I would be a burden to him. It's enough of a struggle looking after you and I'm not ready to look after his family. I don't even know them they are hardly my kin.

166

Crying overtook her again like a fit her thin frame shaking. And I think it is harder than she knows. I remember the first letters we received from my brother John the community he described seemed a primitive one and the climate unforgiving. That they had wet heat and dry infertile soil with all the seasons falling at the wrong time. He wrote of sicknesses doing the rounds and taking many away who were only newly arrived. Though that were some years ago now and it may be that circumstances have improved.

She wept until I felt embarrassed in her presence and thought I should not be there. I let her be left her rocking to herself the sobs coming more controlled. She is a hard woman this state will leave her. I do not quite believe she feels everything she says. If the suffering were real it would be enough to spur her to go. She claims to be unhappy here but she will not change well perhaps she has grown too close to her unhappiness she clings to it for comfort like a child to a blanket and will not lay it down.

I went into my room took up the Bible to read but did not have much concentration for it. *Australia* kept coming to my mind. The word summons up great things for me the promise of adventure when I am sick and tired of everything here I know too well.

38

The last week of November were one of colourless winter light when it seemed as though everything were dressed in grey. The landscape is bare and rough. Winter has come like a thief to spirit the life from it. A drab unblemished skin of cloud above us reaching to the horizon at every point we have not seen the sun.

In the afternoons I have begun to make enquiries for new lodgings. She would not go to her son my landlady she were too unprepared to think so grandly too set on the pettiness of living but it is not the right place for me it has been a trouble I have endured too long. I have increased my visiting because it has provided me an excuse to be away from my lodgings I cannot stand it there. So I have asked at chapel and enquired of visitors to the forge I know Mr Coad has listened to me while I talked there but he did not intervene and has said nothing on the matter. Well I had been thinking there might be some room for me there beside the forge I need only a small space and a bed I am often away with duties. But perhaps that were too optimistic he has a family and I would not fit there.

Still I have some hope I might find somewhere cheaper or a place that is closer to work. Somewhere more comfortable might suit me a Christian house more generous with its warmth. I have given her the news that I will be moving out though I have not yet found a room it seemed fair to give her warning so that she is able to look for a replacement. It seemed the right thing to do even though it might come back against me and I could find myself with nowhere to stay at all. I am not sure what she thinks of it I can do no right with her you would have thought for all her complaints she would be glad I were leaving but it felt like her disapproval were still in place just the same as ever.

Well I do not greatly care I have had larger troubles on my mind.

I feel that I am torn and pulled by conflicting desires and no solution presents itself to me. I am called home to be a part again of that belonging I had as a child I am called away to new lands. I am called to the Church for hope of my own Salvation I am driven from it. I have no security here no means to put a shape on my life or give it my own design. I cannot clear my head.

How swiftly a little illness leads my spirit to be depressed and my mind to linger on black thoughts. I do not understand how it is I come so quickly to feeling a longing for death whenever that sickness returns to me. Seems I am not strong enough even to bear a few minutes of it. Oh the glories awaiting us may be great enough but I will not lie to myself it is escape from this life I covet. I cannot abide to suffer not even if that suffering were *his* will it does not feel it is. And though that death is half-desired still I am saddened to tears at the thought of leaving this world. There has been a Heaven here and it has been lost why should I long for a new one.

I have had some relief from the sickness in recent weeks but it has not gone entirely I think it is tied to the unhappiness I have been feeling. The numbness that sets in me when I come to worship. A terrible lack of feeling where there has been such joy previous. Why is it that such a good and simple thing can impart such dejection to my soul? Some days I feel that to persist with the Church would kill me or mean an end to my faith entirely. I have taken myself from it because I could not breathe there but the freedom of my own breath may be too much. The cold clean air. I know I suffer from the want of social communion the body that binds the Church together.

My Master says *I am the way* but I do not know if I walk *his* path still or if I have strayed from it the way is narrow too narrow. The Lord commands fellowship for *he* comes where we are called to gather. And I feel as though I have been damned because I cannot abide that fellowship yet I believe my faith will not survive without it. The Church is lodged in me like a fishbone in my throat I cannot be rid of it but it threatens to choke me. Or it is a hard stone pressed always smaller and harder though I am shaken. It is grit and blood and loss. And all this while the tide of my faith retreats drawing back over the rough sands and leaving me by the shallows cut off from the land and the ocean both and unwilling to stride forth for either.

Oh I will stride forth. The West burns in my mind the promise of better things elsewhere. I have said strange unkind words to James I think they were a result of my recent sickness it has twisted my feelings about many things and I must straighten them out. He gave me the hope of fellowship is my close friend and understands me better than I have admitted. I could go to him. I long to be away from my troubles here at times there would seem to be nothing so easy as departing for a new home elsewhere. As though the simple fact of distance could cure me. But I could have no new life with it.

I miss my family I long for home.

I need be away from here.

I have sought to retrace in me the strong cord of faith I have known I have been thinking back to my conversion and tried to return that feeling. But I am not sure I understand what it were. I can hardly imagine it now.

It has been near five years since that class meeting there has been no happier day in my life. I have failed to record an account of it and I must correct that. I knew what I felt then I have never claimed to understand it fully it were a *mystery* certainly but then it were a mystery which fulfilled me.

We had a speaker that night a missionary who had been in distant lands I did not recognize the names of the places he spoke of. But he were a local man though born and bred in the Tamar Valley and schooled in our chapels. I thought how strange it were that God had led him on such a journey and returned him to us at the end of it. He provided a powerful testimony about the work of the Lord in foreign lands though they were strange places as I imagined them I could not believe them to be entirely real.

At the end of his testimony our man called forth the Holy Spirit to touch our hearts and speak to us and for those of us who were saved to stand and join him. I were not the first to stand. I did not expect to be the one called I thought my house were already well ordered and would not be visited by our Saviour that night I were only curious to see who among us would be that I could praise God for them. I thought myself to be already in the fold. Well it transpired that it were my door *he* came to and I unprepared for it. I sat in that row of men and a great peace came over me something profound as though someone kind had leant over and rested their hand on my shoulder as though to say *All is well*. And I knew in my heart. I knew it as I have known nothing before or since.

And did not my heart roar within me while I talked with *him* and has *he* not opened *his* scriptures to me? Bible Christians in the West have been known to weep and howl and dance. Well I have often been afraid for what fills them but it may be joy. No such thing is unseemly in the sight of the Lord. I did not dance that night but the change in my heart caused it to leap and the blood coming through were as song to me.

So I received my call. And then two years later I were called again this time to be a vessel for my Master to have *his* Word in me and let it run through me. That Word has transported me I have given myself over to it and have required no other direction. I preached it as it came it were a living Gospel and seemed a tremendous privilege. I spoke the Word as it were revealed to me it were told in uncommon language strange to my simple tongue but it came easily then and it comes no more. It were a mystery but an uncomplicated one that required no explanation of itself.

What should I do then now that confidence I had in it is waned? Should I speak those few truths that have settled in my heart and try to find an explanation of them? Should I preach but feel nothing of it in my stomach save a sickness? I have known the Word long enough to create the semblance of conviction I can put on an act and preach as many words as people may wish to hear but what use were that if they are not true? They would be ashes on my tongue no better than lies the taste of them bitter and sickening. I would rather lose my life in battling for the truth than in preaching death and deceit feeling the ruin and shame of it deep inside me.

Well perhaps this will not endure. Perhaps the Word will come fresh and renewed and I will find truth among my doubts too. But I cannot coerce it from me and though it is whole and made of flesh my heart seems broken it will not suffer that now. I am tired tonight and full of doubt in everything. I do not know what it is I need. All these desires I speak of fall away and I cannot bring myself to want any of them.

39

Though I kept it well fed the fire in the forge has burned low this week folded back by the cold its flames suppressed. I have persevered with the bellows so we have had the right heat to work with but it has been dark as iron inside the smithy and I have worked in shadow feeling half dissolved into the blurring surrounds my eyes becoming insensible to the world. Just that centre of bright heat to focus them and the showering sparks thrown out to be extinguished on the dirt floor. Shadows skittering close around the fire metal sounds shaping the darkness beyond. I have worked among tools left lying like cast-off limbs parts of me I had set aside. I have laboured amidst the dirt every smut of it familiar to me a reminder of the hours I have spent here.

I have worked on farm tools restoring ploughs to sharpness I have cast horseshoes and good axe blades I have beaten flat a mangled shovel. I have helped Mr Coad shape the iron rims of cart wheels we were preparing for a wheelwright in Liskeard. It has been a good education these weeks I have spent valuable time with my employer seems there is much still to be learned. It takes just forge hammer and anvil to fashion the world he says. And I am proud of my new skills in this craft I feel at last that my industry is being rewarded.

It feels though that I have come to be possessed by this place that the hours spent here have brought me into *its* ownership taking me into a strange debt and further from the freedom I have desired. And my spirit is not what it were the work is different now. Seems more draining. I am become more cautious in it must give more of my hours to achieve the same amount done. I used to be sure in my limbs but I do not have that power any longer. Perhaps this too is education of a kind.

I have wanted to talk to Mr Coad but did not find the opportunity.

I saw William today. He were walking on the road to Menheniot as I returned from work. Came by a corner and there he were a thin outline strolling along moving briskly to keep warm I could not imagine what he were doing here so far from home and even further from the quay. I stopped to let him approach. Saw that he had a worker's bag slung behind him. He were dressed in an adult's clothes too big for him the bottoms of his trousers rolled up and the waist tied tight around him with fraying string the jacket swamping his scrawny frame. I thought it must be one of his father's old suits that Mrs French had kept for him. He appeared lost in thoughts and did not see me standing there until he were very close. Then the carefree look disappeared from his face and his hands came from his pockets he did not greet me.

William I said. It's good to see you. We haven't seen you in class lately I am sure you are missed.

He did not answer we stood quietly a moment in the cold and dark until I felt obliged to press the conversation I struck a cheery tone.

I am sure your friends would be glad to see you back if you came. Don't you miss them?

How are you keeping? I asked. I called by your mother and missed you.

But he remained sullen and quiet. I wanted to mention Harr. I thought it might do him some good if we could speak of her and remember her I am sure he missed her.

Where have you been? I asked instead. My voice were sharper more insistent for an answer.

He lowered his head let it loll down and to the side it were the action of a sulking child reminded me how young he still were.

I am labouring now.

Your mother said so. She told me you were working at the quay.

I am. I was. I've had chores to do he said he gestured to the road behind him.

For your mother?

He looked up at me.

Aye he said. What of it?

He had been shadowed in the poor light of dusk. But my eyes focussed on him more clearly now and I saw that his face and clothes were smeared with dirt. I imagined for a moment he had fallen on his way through the woods but the stains were not of that colour. Not the brown of earthy mud but black instead the exact cast of ash and oil from the pits.

Would you lie to me William?

Again that same gesture of his head I have seen him do previously neither a nod nor a shake. A faint tilt to the side his chin quivering. And it riled me a little his behaviour seemed impolite.

You're just a boy. What are you doing? Your mother has lost a husband and a daughter already you need be there for her. The mines are not for you. It is terrible work and dangerous you should not be so selfish.

You've no say he said. You don't know how things are.

I know that she asked you not to.

You don't know. You used to come all the time and you still don't know. And you've nothing to come for now. You won't come no more.

He spat down in front of me then a full gob of spit which landed at my feet a sudden and violent action. It were a shocking thing. I bent forward to grab him fully possessed of the intent to strike him provide him a sound beating for his behaviour but I have been slow since my illness and he were quick in dancing back. He paused there and watched me I half admired his bravery in not fleeing he knew I would hurt him if I could. But my legs felt numb and heavy and too filled with fatigue to move. Seemed as though I were fixed to the road.

He watched the workings of anger in my face. Then he

continued to back away from me and ghosted from the path disappearing into the dusk.

Well I were furious at him I thought he were in sharp need of some punishment that perhaps he had lacked for too long in his life the discipline by which we learn not to destroy ourselves. *Chasten thy son while there is hope* we are told and perhaps that hope were already gone. But I were saddened too. Sad and weary for him. For his family had endured so much loss and it seemed the strand that held him to his mother were cotton-fine that he stood to lose both her and his own life too. So I thought what a curious kind of freedom it were that he had mocked me with. He had stood like a man in front of me as though he were free to treat his mother this way and act as he pleased and yet his freedom would not save him.

So I went on my way still angry but wondering too if I had failed him if there were anything I could have done for him sooner. And though I did not know what that might have been still I were caused to feel very downcast.

40

We are well into December now today were the 18th and it has brought another Sabbath for us. In the morning I set out for chapel but did not reach it. By St Germans I saw a notice regarding passage to Australia and looked at it a long time. Made a few calculations regarding my wage and what I stood to gain or lose though it were wasted thought I knew I did not have what were required. Such opportunities will not be available to me for long and I need finish my apprenticeship first. And I found after that I could not go on to chapel just stood there quite at a loss about what to do with myself until eventually I returned home and slept the extra hours.

In the afternoon I set out again walking towards the quarterly preachers' meeting though I had no heart for it. And I were halfway there before I came to think about what I were doing and it made no sense to me. Every step I took in the direction of the chapel seemed to heighten my unease and turn my stomach. It is a shameful thing to feel so much distaste towards the house of the Lord and I were disgusted at myself but could not continue on that way my body would not have it.

I thought then that I were not so far from the forge so I went to call by on Mr Coad so that the journey were not entirely wasted. I thought I might talk with him a little about my progress and perhaps he would have some good news for me that we might come to a new arrangement between us.

Well there is no work on the Sabbath the forge were empty and lacking for activity the door pulled fully across. It looked a meagre structure a fragile shelter and it appeared a depressing sight offering nothing save the cold promise of labour.

Beside it though the smith's own cottage were inhabited I heard the happy sounds of family coming from it as I stepped towards the door. It were a strangely dispiriting noise seeming to represent both security and wealth two things I have felt to be lacking from my own life. I suppose they are what I have sought in my work at the forge but it does not feel as though they will ever be mine.

So I grew less sure of myself as I approached the door I did not know what I would say or how I could explain my presence on the Sabbath. The words would not come and the strength I had felt for having that conversation seemed to desert me. I feel like I am owed a great deal but it does not seem that Mr Coad is the one who owes it to me and there is nothing I might fairly claim from him. I stood there and did not knock I walked away.

I turned instead to the east made a much longer journey than I had planned walked all the way to Burraton to visit Mr Pendray. It had been a long time since I were there.

The days are tapering ever shorter I walked into the darkening east with nothing but my memory of the path to guide me in the early evening haze. My legs are still not fit for such activity they protested the journey a thin blade of pain working at the back of my knee. Had I somewhere closer to go to I would have gone.

I were exhausted when I arrived and it were quite late it took a long time for the door to be opened and my Godfather seemed surprised to see me but not displeased. He welcomed me in asked what I were doing in Burraton but I could not say. He were slow to turn round and lead me in it were an effort on my part to stand those extra moments.

He had been returned a long time from the evening service and were preparing for bed. But he were kind enough to sit with me let me fetch some water to drink from a jug in the kitchen. I lit some candle stubs for us. He asked nothing of me but as we sat at the table I could not hold the words back they tumbled from me beyond my control.

I used to pray when I awoke I said. *He* were the first thought in my mind each morning. And when I had finished my work for the day my thoughts returned to *him*. At night I would pray until I slept it were the natural way of things. And now it has ceased in me. I wake and remember that the previous night I have forgotten my prayers just gone straight and sinful into dream.

He listened to me nodded as I spoke. I am sure he were sympathetic but I required an answer from him.

I cannot preach now I said. How can I?

Doubt is the beginning of faith. The path is narrow you know this. I have heard you preach on it.

Yes. But I did not feel it then.

Christ doubted too.

Well I am not Christ.

But *he* were man. The Gospels say that in Gethsemane *he* knew doubt and still *he* died for us. I am not telling you anything you do not know.

If I know it I do not feel it.

For now perhaps. It will not last. They are passing things feelings we should not rely on them for truth.

But what else do we have? I thought. It seemed I had waited long enough already for the Lord to revive his work in my heart. My Godfather might assure me it would return but I felt no faith in him either.

I am afraid I said finally it came out like a confession jumping too swiftly from my lips I had not meant it to carry such weight of feeling.

I see that he said he knew me too well. I cannot change it. Your fears are your own to face. But you have found encouragement in the Lord before.

I do not think I can endure this fear without that encouragement.

Yes. It is possible. For a while. Even doubt will not endure the Light of God.

And what if I never regain that knowledge I once had?

And as I asked that question my heart full of doubts leapt inside me with another: *Were it ever even knowledge?*

What is it you fear? he asked the question coming like a sigh.

Too many things. I am afraid of sickness. For the feel of it and what it does to me. It changes me I do not like it I cannot control the run of my thoughts. I am afraid of not seeing my family again. For my material situation I do not have enough income to make a proper living.

Your apprenticeship is nearly done you will be earning soon. *He* will provide for you and you will find ground for your faith.

My Godfather were tiring as he said it he had been listening to my troubles for too long I felt ashamed. But my troubles would not leave me I could not help myself.

He closed his eyes. He sat peaceful almost impossibly still. His hair were unruly but so soft and white he appeared as I imagine the prophets might have looked it gave him a gentle aspect of sleeping or death.

My head felt hot and dizzy I sensed the rush of time past me. Life jerking on in unnumbered heartbeats. Uneven seconds stolen from us and each one to be repaid in dust soon too soon. Feels like I am already passed into another world. *That which is far off and exceeding deep who can find it out.*

The few candles we had stuttered and gave out. I thought his eyes were tired that he did not realize how dark it were how it settled around us. Perhaps he hid from me how bad his sight had become. The minutes died around us I felt weak as though my life bled from me. Then he stirred and seemed to wake and I saw that though he were old he were filled with the Spirit that in his quietness he still burned for the Lord.

In the gloom he looked up I could hardly discern it. The depth of shadow apparent now to him too.

I got up and went out to fetch a lamp. Lit it for us and brought the light back in.

He were awake then. Fixed me with a clear stare. And in the lines of his face I read a thousand things I did not know there were wisdom folded in every crease I were made to feel terribly ignorant. There were so much he understood that I did not and I felt mocked by it. I thought I would never learn such things that they would remain beyond me.

I will not be like unto him.

He knew sorrow for things beyond my imagination.

When he dies he will have glory still on his lips.

We should pray he said.

My Godfather were old and stiff and not so easily moved as he once were but he stood from his chair and made as though to kneel with me. I helped him down placed a cushion beneath his knees and held his shoulders to keep him strong and balanced. We locked our grasps as though embracing held each other at arms' length his hands behind my neck. We bowed our heads our foreheads near touching. And in this way we knelt together on the floor and prayed there his voice low and persistent speaking in the sibilant tongue of angels.

And I knew my faith were still there a hard kernel inside of me but deep inside and diminishing. Faith is a stone I could forget were there and live with always and not know what the oppressive weight in me were. I were tired and my body sick. I felt I would soon be old. My soul withered and seemed to withdraw from the words as we spoke them. There were force to the prayer but it appears that doubt and disbelief have visited me like a shuddering gale brought from far out to sea and I have been caught in open ground with no shelter to come into.

I looked for my faith I think I saw where it were and would have reached for it had I felt I owned the will but I were afraid.

It were too late to move on I stayed the night there. Mr Pendray found a blanket for me and I stayed in the chair it meant an uncomfortable night but I were tired enough to get some sleep and very glad to feel I were not far from company.

And I have discovered today I left my hat there when I stayed with him well it is an annoyance but next weekend is Christmas and I will go home so it will have to wait until the New Year.

41

Saturday when I woke I were cold beneath my blankets. I
were grateful I did not have to work but could return to visit
my family it pains me to think that my situation has not
allowed me home more often. I have waited a long time for
the blessing of *his* Word that I might return there and it is
finally come. And though I have reminded myself I am here
in *his* service and must take what *he* provides it is somewhat
cold comfort presently.

It were hard to begin moving to dress and find some
warmth. The air were wet and cold in the room a clamminess
hung there with my breath becoming part of it. On the outside the window were finely patterned in ice it were quite
beautiful the frost splayed in an intricate design as though
there were some message in it if I but knew how to read the
signs. The glass felt hot to the touch and sharp it nipped like
an animal at my fingers.

I ate a simple breakfast with my landlady just bread soaked
in hot broth from the tea-kettle and wished her the blessings
of the season before I left. We sat close to the stove crowding
within the small sphere of warmth there and made arrange-
ments for when I would be gone and how much I would owe
her for the time I were away. She told me I were expected to
pay regardless of where I were on a given night I am sure she
were referring to the previous week when I had stayed in
Burraton well it were hardly an intentional absence on my
part and I do not know where she thought I had been. I am
not obliged to answer to her. I thought she must be still angry
at me for telling her I were leaving well there is no satisfying
her. But it were hard not to be cheerful with her I were so
pleased to be coming home the thought had awoken some

hope in me. And I felt for her that she did not have a family who would return. The box of letters she had from her son were open on the shelf I suppose she had been up early reading from them and put them back when she heard me moving. I know it is good to be with loved ones this time of year.

Outside the air were sharply cold but I breathed of it deeply welcoming it into my lungs as though it were happiness itself. I could hardly see the way my eyes blurred with the shock of freezing air I blinked at it but my sight would not clear. I needed to set a brisk pace to raise some warmth my knees never did find it. The cold came at me around my head I regretted the absence of my hat. It caused a sharp ache at the back of my neck like someone pressing a hot iron there. It kept a solid grip on my skull it closed its fist steadily and I were reminded of the firm hand of my father so it came as a blessing of sorts.

The way appeared muddy but that mud were frozen and solid. The grass yellowed in patches a pleasing crunch of ice beneath my shoes the land frosted and bare but still breathing. A gentle rise and fall to it as I walked. The horizon close and lined with leafless trees.

The sky were a watered blue so pale it turned to white then transforming pink in the brief afternoon and copper-clad at sunset as I were arriving home. I followed the cart track across the fields approaching the farm found it pleasing to watch the familiar shapes of the land shifting into view. Passed by the copse of beech trees I used to play in as a child where we each had our own tree my brothers and I our own perch for our games. Mine a worn seat between two low boughs the wood so smooth it seemed it had been polished by generations before me. My brothers always higher up in the thinner branches they were older and braver and established their superiority in this fashion but they needed to cling on carefully to their precarious nests. Mine were a comfortable place for a boy in summer. But the trees are now ivy-shagged just huddled together in the dark cold it seemed absurd that a

solitary place once held such meaning for me. There were a
flash of remembering which told me these things had once
been precious but that I were only a child then and owned
them no more.

At the end of the road our farmhouse cottage. It is walled
from even bricks made of stone with no slate and creeper-
bound on its southern side. The heavy thatched roof sagging
a little in the middle and appearing worn there too it seemed
as though it would need re-thatching in the spring. Stunted
chimneys at either end which none the less appear to stand
proudly marking the high ends of the house. The roof droops
so low over the second floor the windows appear as though
they have been hung from the trimmed edge of the thatch.
And those windows firmly shuttered for winter so I were left
to wonder how many panes of glass remained behind them.

My movements were all stiff and when I made it into the
warmth of home it were a while before I could speak straight
my jaw had grown numb in the frozen air and everything I
said came out a mumble. I were thankful I had not had call to
be out there longer. In the kitchen a fire were lit for my return
and it would be the first time I had been properly warm this
winter. I remember this hearth it were the centre of my life for
many years and sometimes it feels as though my entire life
were born of it. As a child I lived close to it came here for
warmth in the winters. Then when I had begun to work on
the farm it were this grate and the waiting meal that brought
me back in from the land at the end of each day. Seeing it now
has reminded me of many early memories which have been
allowed to escape. The sight of my mother in the kitchen
dressed for church and fussing around us. The company of
the old collie dog we kept who having earned his place by
loyalty and hard work both were allowed to sleep here by the
embers. I remember the stale odour of his coat as it heated up
the stench mingling with more pleasant scents from the
kitchen and the thickening smell of clothes drying by the fire-
side after my mother had washed them in the trough. And

185

stronger than all of these the distinct smell of our own wood burning smoke from the elm and ash we cut down and chopped into logs then left piled behind the house to dry.

My brothers were there to welcome me. Tom who is closest to me in age and Simon the second eldest they have both stayed to work the farm. John of course were missing he has gone to Australia but the last news from him were good apparently. George the middle brother of our five is not yet returned Simon told me that he were arriving the following day bringing his new wife with him perhaps. He has become a policeman and is required tonight for that labour well I suppose there must be someone who keeps order. I have witnessed myself that it is a much needed task but it is hardly the Lord's work. He may set straight the worst of their sins but I do not think we will have much progress if we do not begin with righting their souls.

And then my mother coming down from the upper floor where she had been preparing our beds for us. Slow on the stairs but appearing well less thickness to her than I recalled.

Well she said in greeting. And hasn't it been a long time.

A year. I have been away a year and no miles keeping me just the days filled with work and duties and my inability to fulfil them. But there were no real reproach to her voice just gladness to see me. I hugged her tightly felt the sharpness of her bones and were reminded how long it had been since I had felt contact with someone and how much in need of it I were it felt good. She were happy to see me here but I know her well and it were apparent that the thought of her two sons who were still away were almost as strong.

You seem tired she said. Have you been ailing?

A little sickness I said. Then a cold walk today. But I am well. And you?

Oh. I am getting older.

That at least were clear upon seeing her. Her face appeared creased and worn I am sure she would seem to be an old woman to those who did not know her. Crow's feet evident by her eyes a strange and ugly name for the lines but she is quite beautiful. Her face more weathered by sun than I remember. She is constantly washing her dry hands together to nurse the stiffness there.

How strange to see her. I am happy of course it is greatly reassuring to return and find that this life continues well without me. But I think my closeness to her will always keep me from knowing her fully. I were fed at her breast and though it were my brothers who showed me the work of the farm it seems that everything I have learned about this land has come from her. She knew the names of the trees and the birds taught me to recognize the flowers at the wayside. It were her finger which drew out for the child I once were the patterned stars in their constellations and she who told me which light would be where as the seasons turned. In late summer nights she foretold the coming weather by looking for the clarity of certain parts of the sky. It is a knowledge I have tried to refresh in me I have not ceased to be amazed by the wonders of this world.

She asked about my work and who I had been seeing. Were very pleased that I had seen something of James she had heard he had been back with his family. I told her a little about the forge how it has been there I talked about some of the sick I had visited. I said nothing of anything that troubled me. Did not wish to burden her with it. I wondered if I had already mentioned something of it in my letters well she did not ask.

We ate dinner together the four of us and I experienced the pleasure of company it has been a long time since I knew it. We had a good meal generously portioned a feast for this prodigal son returned well it is my *time* I have been wasteful with. Our conversation were kept busy with the exchange of our news and talk of far-flung places and the lives of my brothers. Tom spoke of the farm and the changes the last year had brought. It stills you to work with the land his conversation comes slow and considered. Feels like he always keeps something back. That he cannot fully express himself to me now that I have left and turned to new labours. Simon barely talks at all his thoughts seem to have slowed to Nature's long pace. They had little to say that did not concern the farm. Simon apparently is courting a girl he would not say anything of her just blushed a little as Tom mentioned it I think he said it to tease him. John is married in Australia I do not think we will ever see her. And George is married too I wonder if she will come with him tomorrow.

The hours passed swiftly I regretted having come so late having tarried for so long in the morning with Mrs Grose. Late on we gathered and dressed in heavy coats walked down through the cold to St Eve chapel for the Watchnight service. Heard a short sermon from Paul's second epistle to the Corinthians 6th Chapter *Behold now is the day of Salvation.*

Something must be done for the circuit the congregation were good as it should be for Watchnight but my mother said it were not always that way. On the Sabbaths there were far fewer just representatives of the local families and a few elderly ladies beside and membership down. I were much embarrassed when the collection plate were brought round and I had nothing to put in it. And it were not that I had merely forgotten to bring a few coins with me but that I had nothing spare to give. The little I had been able to save up in the previous weeks I had put aside for my family. I felt greatly ashamed. It would not have been so bad if the plate were full then people would not have noticed if one person or another did not contribute to the sum but the collection were small when it reached me. I passed it on without adding a penny. I am sure I reddened. The collecting steward did not look up he were kind enough to act as though he had not seen it.

I listened to the sermon I did not turn against it. I nodded in agreement with the Word. I sang the same hymns and felt a little of their old power. For a moment my spirits lifted. Provided me the sense of being briefly unburdened. We sang our last hymn in stirring voice and sounded in Christmas Day.

After the service we shared greetings with our neighbours. I were introduced to a girl the daughter of one of the church members who were a friend of my mother. She were very polite. We had a pleasant conversation about the sermon. But later when my heart should have been taken up with praising God and when I should have been refreshed in my spirit I felt downcast. There were a darkness in my soul and I wondered what spirit or sadness possessed me what I were thinking of. That depression seems to wait for me in God's house well tonight I have had my family present and I think they have provided some insulation from it but I will not have them here for long.

We walked home in the freezing night it were too cold to speak. No cloud to envelop us just cold into the heavens the stars painful clear. A bright meteor lighted up the element over our heads. Praise God it is not all dark.

I slept well in an old bed enjoyed the warmth of a decent quilt and for once my dreams seemed warm too. Then woke to a twice blessed day it is not often I remember Christmas falling on a Sabbath. I rose early and took up my chores. Hauled provender for the beasts. Split some wood to add to the log pile searched for the driest pieces to bring in then took the small bellows to sharpen the fire.

George and his wife Elizabeth arrived in time for chapel. She is a stern woman but pleasant enough she did not like the necessity of travelling on the Holy Day but I did not see what else they could do he needed work Christmas Eve and it is surely better that they be with their family today than sit home merely because they thought it would be improper to go out. She has a habit of standing behind my brother I found her difficult to talk to and George seemed subdued in her company.

Our morning service were given over to carols with not much of a sermon accompanying. It is tradition and I do not mind the carols though I find there is something childish about them and consequently they are a little painful to endure. The children enjoy them well enough but they seem insubstantial fare to me. They evoke the season though and because we do not come to them often there is a certain novelty to it. But I prefer the old hymns Wesley's hymns that we have the remainder of the year.

I sat with George and Elizabeth she has a rather thin voice quite high with not much substance to it. After we had been blessed I remarked to George how good it were to have the family back together.

We have not heard from John he said.

I thought there had been good news from him I said.

Aye but it were months back he is normally better at writing.

It is hardly a short distance for the letters to come. There's plenty that could delay them. He will be well. We would know it if not don't you think?

Perhaps.

I suppose this is how things are. We are called away to our own labours regardless of reach. Such distances are strange things unimaginable ideas which cannot be envisaged by us for our minds do not have the capacity and are happier with distances they can see and comprehend.

And so this is how things are I am back among my brothers whom I know so well. We played together and worked together we are from the same home the same earth and I feel close to them. But I feel also that a change has taken place since I were called away from here although they are looking much the same as when I last saw them on their outsides at least. So perhaps the change is in *me* and I have come to look at them differently since I went away.

We have had our Christmas meal shared out a goose which had been cooked slow while we were at church I have not had such food for a long time its richness were overwhelming. One topic of conversation we returned to as we ate were that of Australia I think my mother would have been glad for some news of John well it would not come today. I considered whether to say I had been thinking of seeing out my apprenticeship and emigrating myself but I did not know how they would take it. I decided to talk to Tom alone later and see what his reaction were before spreading the idea wider it hardly seemed realistic now. And I am sure it were not best to return home after so long away only to say I were going to leave. No doubt they still see me as the infant of the family and my going would be a very different thing from what John's departure had been.

I have said before that I am the youngest of our brood well it is not quite the truth. We had a little sister who died just after she were born she had a name but did not last long enough to grow into it. She has no separate grave we did not have the money but were buried in with our father's parents their grave reopened for her. Nothing added to the headstone though when I am there I imagine her name written on it I do not see why she should not have that right.

Well my mother is proud of her boys but she would have liked a girl too. And she could have no more children after that so I were the last and I think that the death were a great revelation for her. If my sister had survived she would never have known her father he died soon after and were interred but a few feet distant.

The years after my father died were hard on my mother. We have all struggled for security in our time circumstances will make things hard for us. Though the actual ache of his passing does not trouble me so much now I think of him often and having returned home I have been mourning his loss it is a powerful reminder of his hold on my life. I have a favourite verse from the parables of Christ in the Book of Luke 15th Chapter *I will arise and go to my father* it says and it seems to me that we are all come after our fathers and no doubt we go to follow them too.

So late in the afternoon when the boys were out on the farm and the remainder of us gathered downstairs I found myself settling in the corner of the room my father had used as his study years before. The writing desk there with the family Bible laid on it. A few of his books still arranged in a row though I do not know that he read them much. It would have been a slow struggle for him. I do not remember being called to read for him neither and though the books are worn their spines are unbroken. Perhaps he knew enough to respect all this paged knowledge but felt that it were not for him. There were not much there. Some works of commentary. An edition of Wesley's *Notes on the New Testament* a few teetotaller pamphlets old tracts against drinking and these finally thumbed with use there were some that had been written on with sentences underlined. My father liked to mark those texts he agreed with most strongly perhaps he saw future use for those passages in his sermons. I think his instinct though in this were good our reading becomes a part of us and if we do read then we should strive to read moral and instructive works.

I sat at that desk long hours until the clock struck and recalled me to the kitchen. My mother is no longer so nimble with her tasks and only Elizabeth there to help her no daughter of her own. They had prepared a simple meal between them and we ate quietly sensing that the brief holiday were already done with. My mother were attentive to Elizabeth I think she were sharp aware that she had four sons here and all of us grown men yet only one of us with a wife. I wonder if she is disappointed in us.

I slept well again enjoyed a second night cocooned in warmth regretted very much leaving that bed when I woke. Well it has been the happiest time I have had for long months and I have felt quite prone to sudden changes of emotion. I have not felt entirely comfortable here it is strange to come back to a farm where I no longer work. The chores felt both natural and awkward to my body. But I have been shaking with longing for it I have felt *at home* here part of that old sense has reared up to welcome me back.

Still it is not all happiness for I have been gone too long and it is only now I have seen how old my mother is become. I wish I had had better news of myself to give to her. She has told me she has not been well in recent months well I wish she had written to me about it I might have found the time to visit. Tom has told me that she fell last week on the stone kitchen floor and could not get up on her own he found her there some time after. Well she has waved it away and did not mention it to me herself but hearing of the incident caused me much fear and a thought to arise in me that I cannot keep away. That those I have known and loved all my life will grow old and sick and stranger to me.

George left early Monday morning he and Elizabeth took a cart we did not have much time to say goodbye. Tom and Simon were out at work before I had risen. When I talked to Tom the previous night he advised me to write to John in Australia so that he might better order my thoughts on what it might mean to go there. Well perhaps in the new year I will.

I saw my mother in the kitchen ate breakfast with her and gave her the money I had set aside. I held her in a hug almost lost her in my arms I did not hold her too tight for fear of crushing her.

Stay close to God she said.

And then those two days were done with they had sparked quickly in my heart and burned there with a flaring heat remaining only to cool.

The path home were the same path that I have walked before yet each step seemed to be false and one made in the wrong direction. Yet I felt I had no other way to go. The cottage waiting for me at Quethiock had not changed my room were bare and cold the same as I left it. It seems as though I have had no other life than this one here.

42

The days still come. What will they contain now. Another year is near to eternity and I thank the Lord I have been spared to see the new one arrive I trust I will be more faithful than in the one that is gone. I am called to think on the changes it has brought many have exchanged worlds some have fallen from grace or have left their homes for foreign lands and some are laid on beds of sickness. All these things speak to us they say there is no time for mirth nor trifling here.

It is New Year's Eve and cold in my room as I do my accounts. I have two candles lit and my blanket taken up from the bed and set around my shoulders. The sound of church bells carries clear in the night marking the close of a service I did not attend.

I could not bring myself to suffer company tonight. Feels I am not yet ready to return to the chapel. So I have turned instead to my accounts to weigh up what I have given and I have found myself in debt to the Lord I have not contributed all that I promised at the beginning of the year so now I have cause for more labour. My apprenticeship embarrasses me I know I am older than is usual I should be married and moved on in life. Well I have chosen late I trust God will provide or else *he* shall call for me and I will have nothing to show.

But the reckoning of earthly matters has been quite tedious tonight and I have found myself longing instead for a system by which I might weigh up my spiritual accounts. I fear that my debts there are still greater and swelling in number. If only our souls were so simply judged. I feel I have slept through the year not awoken from my soul's

194

infatuations. Harr were the salt of the day and her company so sweet to me. And because I have hungered for salvation I were drawn to her light and became so desirous of that perfect state that I lost my own way. I have dreamt the days away as though it were not within my power to order the time. It is small wonder I feel such discomfort before my Master neither can I set foot in *his* house. I need repent of my sins. I need begin anew.

What shall I do then. I may find new lodgings and escape this unhappy house but I will not stray far. What freedom do I have? There is a scattered flock here but it is *my* flock and *my* place I have not lost them yet and will not forsake them. The line of my blood has run in a narrow course these generations and I have no wish to see it branching the channelled blood allowed to thin and dissipate until it runs no more. If the world turns but a little more I am afraid we will lose our families. I will keep close to them and to my friends too. They offer life and warmth and hope. If there is money next year I will visit James and we will see then if we have been lost. I should like to see the West.

My room were cold it would not keep warmth in it. I curled into bed leaving the candles to burn down for whatever reluctant heat they might provide. Closed my eyes to the flickering light and struggled to pray for forgiveness until something like the voice of the Lord came to comfort and accompany me and I were calmed a little feeling more secure. But my concentration were inconstant and the course of the prayer faltered in my mind. I opened my eyes.

The bells still sounded they came discordant across the distance hauling in the early hours of the new year. It were an alluring sound the only sign I had that human life continued tonight. But they called to no one the night were empty. And I saw that there will be no kingdom builded here none of Heaven's glories to limn this earth. The light of Salvation came once like a beam through the night and shone among these hills but the clouds have thickened and I do not see it now. Feels I am much in need of some light.

The bells grew longer. Seemed for a brief moment that they had slowed and dragged time to slowing with them. That I might breathe of it and delay my breathing until I held time itself within my lungs that I could make it pause until I had found its measure and we breathed together. But the slowness of my breath were not enough and still the bells returned their toll strange and ghostly in the night the sound lingering like a wraith among the hills before fleeing. And then silence and the year were gone into eternity. It is a new one now.

The years will not be restored to me. They turn over and run in until all this is gone before they pull life from me I can feel the tugging at my chest and belly and the grievous aching pain. My arms and legs too heavy to draw against it. I know what this feeling is it is loss and it is harrowing and I am afraid. I do not know how I will live with it seems it will take everything from me. Strange how much of an animal I feel myself to be at this moment just flesh and bone encasing an empty core and an instinct to cry out for the loneliness of it. Where is the soul that binds this life together?

And still the days come meted out like water from a drying well. How many more of them shall we have? The days come they number fewer they grow short and I feel how pressing time is. Everything given over to be lost from us. The hours desert us while we still have hold on them and though we open our hands to see what it is we grip we find our hands are empty. This *present* where we live is an impossible point it cannot be. There is nothing other than a falling into eternity our freedom taken from us in the rush of time.

And yet I have felt free in the past so why not now. Each moment must be new. We have them briefly but they have not been lived before. Though they go quickly from us and there is nothing in the days that we have not already seen there must be room for us. Room for decisions and choices room enough for us to be *free* so that we are not condemned to trudge our plotted courses to their end without say on where those roads lead us. Except for our freedom we are all a part of the lifeless Inferno consumed and destroyed by this world. We must have choice. I cannot see it in my life but it must be so. How else shall we be saved?

An account of moneys given to the poor and the cause of God this term.

			£	s.	d.
Sep.	5	to the British and Foreign Bible Society	0	2	6
	18	to the reopening services of Saltash chapel	0	2	6
	20	a packet of tracts	0	1	0
	25	class money	0	2	1
Oct.	2	to the poor	0	1	0
		chapel fund collection	0	0	1
	16	give to the missionary collection	0	2	0
	19	Seat Rents	0	1	0
		to Minnard	0	1	0
Nov.	3	to the poor	0	2	0
	13	to the missionary collection	0	1	0
	23	given to a man out of work	0	0	6
Dec.	12	put into a missionary box	0	1	0
	25	to the missionary cards	0	0	3
		to the poor	0	1	0
	27	to the poor Quethiock	0	3	6
		class money	0	2	1
			1	4	6